he made my mama laugh

By

Lawrence Stripling Sr.

Books-Motion Pictures-Television

FRAZIER PUBLISHING & SERVICES

P.O. Box 363835

North Las Vegas, NV 89036

ISBN-10: 0-9709701-2-9

ISBN-13: 978-0-9709701-2-1

TABLE OF CONTENTS

CHAPTER 1

GRAMMY HAS SO MUCH LOVE TO GIVE

I know people talk about me, I hear them whispering behind my back all of the time. For instance, I overheard my father, aka delinquent daddy; tell his friends at a cookout, that I am an evil little bitch with a nasty attitude. Wow! I love you too daddy. He told his friend Benny that if he ever came up missing or dead, that I either did it or had something to do with it. He believes that I would kill him in his sleep and then tell the world about it. What a silly Negro. If I did kill him in his sleep, I would never tell. Everyone knows that when you kill a person, you never tell a living soul. I hope he's sleeping with one eye open.

Grandmother, that's my father's mother, says that I am foul mouthed and mean spirited. I guess I do cuss a lot, so I'm cool with being called foul moth, but mean spirited? I'm not sure what that means, but if it pisses Grandmother off then I like it.

Grandmother also calls me strong willed. I hear that calling someone strong willed is the same as calling them a bitch. Let me tell you that my Grandmother is very strong willed woman.

Grandmother said to her friend Doris that I inherited her family's good looks and strong features. Then she said it was sad that I inherited my mother's family ghetto mentality and lack of home training. I kicked her on the shin and told her lighten up you mean spirited, strong willed, uppity old goat. I'm just a little kid but I'll be damned if I let you say my mama's family doesn't have home training.

The kids in the neighborhood are terrible. To my face they are like "hi Cola, how are you doing" or "hey girl, nice outfit. Behind my back they call me Cola the coconut or kid crazy. Kid crazy, I love that nickname.

Most of the kids are afraid of me. They know that I will cuss them out or punch them in the face. I don't understand just because you head butt a boy and break his nose and cuss out a prissy girl at her tea party (she's lucky I didn't punch her in the face) and everyone thinks you're crazy, Go figure.

The school psychologist says that I am acting out to get attention from my parents. She claims that I am rebellious because I am the second born. She told my mother that I have what professionals call the middle child syndrome (what's up with this middle child crap? Who do I look like, Jan Brady? Marsha, Marsha, Marsha!).

I found a letter from the psychologist in mamas' room. I swear that I was not snooping, but there in her top drawer between her bras and panties hidden under the bank book was this letter.

It was a long letter with a lot of big words that I didn't understand.

Case number 29357

Subject: Nicola Norwell

Regarding: Behavior problems and possible solutions

Nicola Norwell is from a single parent household. Said child is a loner with signs of anti-social behavior, violent aggressions and self-destructiveness. This behavior I believe is due in fact to the following:

A) No father figure within the home. Father has not lived in the home during past five years. (Parents divorced) Visitation and interaction from father is rare. I have observed a disturbing mutual hatred between the father and said child.

B) Nicola is allowed unrestricted television viewing at all hours of the night. Viewings include vintage gangster movies, soap operas, Betty Davis movies, Alfred Hitchcock movies and a variety of drama related television that is unsuitable for a child her age. This activity has given said child a broad vocabulary, an acute comprehension of adult situations and a flair for the dramatic.

C) Said child's Grandmother on her mother's side is called Grammy. It seems that Grammy has the biggest influence on Nicola. Grammy not only teaches, but encourages Nicola to speak as an adult, use vulgar language and act out her aggressions. Upon meeting Grammy, my first impression was that there was no way this beautiful little lady could be anything like Nicola had mentioned during our sessions. Grammy appeared to be very grandmotherly with a very warm nature and an infectious laugh. Grammy brought me blueberry muffins and a bouquet of flowers. I found Grammy to be a total delight and the muffins were heavenly. As we discussed Nicola and her above average intelligence, she became the doting Grandmother, praising her grandchild and telling cute little stories about Nicola. Such a loving grandmother, I couldn't help but smile. As I cautiously steered the conversation toward the negative influence that I felt Grammy may be having on Nicola, she gasped and seemed to be taken aback. I felt bad, feeling that I may have offended her.

Grammy smiled and asks me to come close. I leaned in like she asked and in a soft soothing voice that was just above a whisper, Grammy calmly cussed me up one side and down the other. That woman said things to me that I have never heard in my thirty-seven years on this earth. Our conversation and her language were too inappropriate to document in my report.

D) As a seventh grader Nicola is reading well above the seventh grade level and has above average intelligence. We are working with her mother, Mrs. Tanya Norwell to encourage Nicola to participate in sports or group activities that would involve children her own age. I have strongly suggested limiting television access and supervised visitation with Grammy. Nicola's mother was very understanding and promised that from this day forward, her daughter's time with Grammy will be supervised by her and the television viewing will be held to a minimum or eliminated altogether.

There was more to the letter, but I couldn't read any more. I felt a lump in my throat and I was about to cry. So I folded the letter and put it back in the drawer.

I couldn't believe what the psychologist wrote about me. What I understood was mostly true. But she wants me to stop hanging out with Grammy that will never happen.

....

Damn, look at me just rambling on. I was telling all my business like you all know who I am. Let me introduce myself. My full name is Nicola Kim Norwell. Everyone calls me Cola. I hate the name Nicola. I will punch anyone who thinks about calling me that. I love my middle name Kim though. I think I look and act like a Kim. So you can call me Kim. My family is just like any other family around our neighborhood. Except Grammy, she is special and I love her to death.

Grammy is the smartest woman that I know. She is even smarter than my mama. Grammy said she is smarter than mama because she is her mother. She taught mama everything she knows. That makes good sense to me and that makes my Grammy the smartest woman ever.

Grammy and I were watching the movie Irreconcilable differences. You know that movie with Drew Barrymore in it where she divorces her parents. I asked Grammy if I could divorce my father and change my name to Kim. She said "Sure you can honey, when you turn thirteen."

I can't wait until I turn thirteen. I'm going to divorce my father but not my mama. My mama is cool. When I divorce my father I'm going to kick him in the balls and tell him to kiss my ass, just like my mama did when they got divorced.

I have one older brother named Michael who is four years older than me and a younger sister Tyreese who is one year younger. I am the middle child but I don't have a middle child syndrome like the psychiatrist said.

We call my baby sister Ty. I tell her the reason we call her Ty is because mama wanted a boy so bad that for the first five years of her life mama would stand her up tall and bop her on the head hoping her rabbit would pop out. You know a penis. So every now and then I bop her on the head and tell her to check to see if her rabbit popped out.

Here I am talking like this story is all about me. Well it's not, it's about my mama. Tanya Norwell is my mama's name. My Mama is very tall, close to six feet and she's beautiful. I would say that she is as fine as four movie stars put together, she looks that good. Mama played basketball and ran track in college so she is in great shape. During the summertime she is the assistant track coach at the high school. Mama's cooking is the best and she bakes pies and cookies all of the time. I bet she can cook and bake better than Betty Crocker and Julia Child combined.

Everyone in the neighborhood loves and respects my mama. She does a lot with the church, helps the elderly and looks out for all the neighborhood kids. She does so much to make sure that everyone is happy that she forgets about herself.

Five years ago mama caught daddy cheating again. Mama was so mad that she got all up in my father's face. I'm talking shouting, shoving and mama swinging. They usually argued at night in their bedroom, but this was the first time in front of us kids. I will remember that day forever. It was right after school in the living room. Mama was screaming and pushing daddy. She asked daddy if he had children by another woman. Daddy looked like he was going to cry when he finally said yes.

Mama punched daddy in the face so hard that she broke his nose.

Daddy broke down; he told mama that he had another woman and two kids living across town. Mama screamed saying that was the final straw and it was too much for mama to deal with. Turns out mama had been bugging daddy for years to have another kid. Daddy sneaking around and having kids with another woman tore mama's heart to pieces. That was the first time in my life that I saw mama cry. Seeing her cry made me cry. I was so mad at my father for making my mother cry that I wanted to punch too. Instead I went to my room and threw things across the room.

The day after their big fight, daddy watched as his friends Mr. Benny and Mr. Todd took his things from the house. He looked pitiful and small.

He called us over and told us that he wouldn't be living with us anymore. He said mama was divorcing him and he would come around whenever he could to see us. This was a shock to us. My daddy was leaving. How could he leave us? Wasn't there some way he could make things right with mama? They fought in past, but they always made up and Daddy never left the house. Did he have to go?

My daddy stood there on the porch and told us that everything would be alright. He said mama would take good care of us, you know, raise us right. He told my brother that he was now the man of the house and to look out for his mama and sisters. He held out his hand to shake and my brother pushed it away.

My brother Michael who at the time was thirteen and almost as tall as my father yelled "Mama doesn't deserve this. My mama is a good person. Everyone loves mama, why couldn't you. You're a coward and a sorry ass father. No one mistreats my mama and no one make my mama cry. Get the fuck off my porch and don't ever come back."

Daddy lowered his head and turned away from Michael.

Daddy looked to me and told me to be good and stop acting out. He reached for me and I stepped back. If my big brother was

6

mad at him, so was I. He made mama cry, he made my brother mad and I was now so mad that I wanted to cry.

He picked Ty up, gave her a big hug and a kiss and told her he loved her. Ty kissed him back. He put her back down on the porch and asked her to go in the house and get her mama.

Ty didn't return and mama didn't come out of the house to say goodbye. Michael and I stayed on the porch.

Daddy looked at us and stepped off the porch. He made it half way down the sidewalk before he turned and spoke. He pointed to a fancy new car that had a white lady in the front seat and two sandy haired kids sitting in the back. He said "those two beautiful children in the car are your brother and sister, when things settle down maybe you can meet them" My brother looked at my daddy in disbelief. He then called him everything but a child of God before storming into the house.

Ty stepped back on the porch. She smiled, waved and told daddy that she was happy to have another brother and sister.

I stood glued to the porch feeling like I was going crazy.

I remembered what Grammy always told us, if someone hurts your mama, your brother or your sister, you hurt them twice as bad.

I was now so pissed I was seeing red. I turned and hugged my little sister and told her to go in the house with mama and Michael. I called for my father in my sweetest little girl voice "daddy, don't go" I said. He turned and smiled; he went down on one knee and opened his arms wide for a hug. I ran down the stairs to him with my arms out for what he thought was a hug. I was about two feet away from him when I jumped up and head butted him right on the nose. I heard a nasty crunch. I stood back and looked at him. His nose was bloody and dripping on the sidewalk. I had hit him in the exact place that mama did the night before. The white woman and the two kids came running out of the car but stopped when they saw blood. The woman told the kids to get back in the car as she watched in terror. I watched her, I watched my father, my fist balled up tight, I was ready for a fight.

I yelled "No one messes with my family."

My daddy stood up dripping blood everywhere and said "shit, I deserved that" then he went to his new family got in the car and drove off.

I was so mad that I stood on the side walk and screamed every swear word I knew until my throat was raw. I didn't cry, I couldn't cry, I refused to cry. Mama had cried enough for all of us. I swore on that day that I would make that bastard pay. He made my mama cry.

Now, here we are five years later and mama still isn't happy, she smiles a lot and makes sure everyone is happy, but she hardly ever laughs and sometimes at night, I can hear her cry herself to sleep. Mama didn't deserve this and she didn't deserve what my daddy did to her. So, each night I pray .... "Lord, please send someone to make my mama happy again; please send someone to make my mama laugh"

CHAPTER 2

THINGS ARE GONNA GET EASIER

"Child, what is wrong with you, don't you know how rude it is to stare at people. Cola, would you please stop looking at that man" mama shook me out of my trance and was talking sternly to me in a hushed voice.

I couldn't help but stare, everything about this man was so different, so unlike my father. If my Grammy were here, she would say "Child, this is the kind of man that would make me lose my religion, for sure. If I were ten years younger he would be your new Granddaddy, let me tell you" Then Grammy would give out a loud laugh, slap her knee, raise her hands to the heaven and ask the Lord for forgiveness.

The stranger was sitting in our favorite restaurant Newton's, five booths away from us reading the newspaper, eating pancakes and drinking coffee. Each time he reached for his coffee he would look at our table, wink, nod his head and give us a warm friendly smile. My little sister Ty would laugh and wave each time he did so and I would just stare. When I looked over at my mother she was seriously mean mugging the dude. Usually that look would send men running in the other direction, but not this man; he lifted his coffee mug to mama and smiled.

"Mama" I said in my innocent child voice "he seems friendly enough and he is very handsome, why you don't just wave back at him or at least say hello" Since my parents' divorce five years ago mama hasn't even looked at another man.

"The gift" told me that this may be the man for my mama.

Let me tell you about "the gift" My Grandma Nicole, that's my father's mother, told me that God has blessed me with "the gift." Grandma Nicole said the gift means that I can see things before other people can see them. She said it was like looking through a window into the future. What am I supposed to see, I don't know? Sometimes I get a feeling that I can't shake and I see things in my brain, things that I know will happen later. I know it sounds crazy to you, but it is even crazier inside my head.

"He must have a death wish, looking at us like that, that's disrespectful. I'm here with my children, trying to have a decent lunch and this clown is flirting, how bold" my mother said to no one in particular.

"The gift" told me that he was meant to be here for us and he was going to be a part of our lives one day. My mother had a look that said otherwise.

If Grammy were here she would have boldly called the man over. She would have told him "Hey honey, no need in staring, this isn't no picture show. Pick up your plate and your coffee and bring your narrow ass on over here. Bring your paper too, I want the coupon section. Don't forget your wallet, because you'll be buying us lunch today and thank you kindly."

....

My name is Nicola Kim Norwell and I am twelve years old. Everyone calls me Cola or Cola Kim, not on account of my skin tone or because I am so sweet and bubbly. They call me this name that I hate with a passion because of my deadbeat daddy. My Grammy told me when I was born mama had some trouble and the doctors drugged her. My daddy was drunk and decided to tell the nurse that he was flirting with, that the name on the birth certificate was to be Nicole Kim Norwell. He named me after his mother. His drunken ass slurred and spelled his own mothers name wrong, so here I am Nicola instead of Nicole. Mama raised five kinds of hell when she came to, because my first name was supposed to be Kim.

Where was I, oh yeah, my gift. I had a very bad feeling that made me cry. I told my Grandmother Nicole that something bad was about to happen to Grandpa Jim. I told her that I saw her telling my father that Grandpa Jim would be leaving us soon. Then a few days later the doctors said Grandpa Jim had cancer. Grandpa Jim passed away three months later.

About a year later my gift brought me another bad feeling. I saw mama crying and she was telling us that daddy was gone. Two weeks later, to everyone's surprise, except mine of course, my father was gone. No, unfortunately he didn't die, even though I tell everyone he did. The bastard walked out the door, down the front stoop and out of our lives.

It was as though he had died and took a piece of my mama with him. My mama has been sad, angry, weak and alone ever since the day he left.

I told Grammy that I wished mama was tougher like her and would just forget about my father. Grammy told me that toughness is not in my mother's nature. She told me I would have to be tough enough for the both of us.

Grammy also told me that if a man ever left her for another woman, he wouldn't be leaving her house with nothing but the clothes on his back and a half pound of buckshot in his ass.

My gift sends me good visions too. I had a vision that my mother and sister were dancing and laughing in the kitchen. This was just a few days after my father left us. This vision really made no sense to me because my mother and sister had been crying and moping around the house since the day dear old dad left. I swear to God, I thought they would never smile or laugh again. Note to self, stop swearing to God.

In the vision I came in from school and I heard the stereo blasting out mama's favorite song "Thanks for saving my life" by a singer named Billy Paul, she had my sister in her arms and they were spinning and laughing all over the room.

When they saw me they scooped me up and we all laughed and danced until I stopped and asked "mama, why are we dancing?" she held my face in her hands and told me that my little sister had very high test scores and the principal put her in for a scholarship at the catholic school around the corner and she was accepted.

I didn't know what a scholarship was, but if it made mama happy, I was happy too. If it meant that my little sister didn't have to go to the nasty ass elementary school down the block, that was cool with me. The school is a shit hole. Hey I'm just repeating what I heard my second grade teacher say. I hated the school, but loved my teachers and all of my friends. My sister didn't have many friends in this school and the kids called her weird. My sister isn't weird, she is just a lot smarter than those jack asses and they are just jealous. OK, so my sister is weird, but I'm the only one who gets to call her that. I'm happy for her and I am sure that she will fit right in with all of the weird kids at the Catholic school.

....

"Damn, what was I talking about again? I done got myself off track. Oh yeah, the man in the diner and the good feeling I had about him"

Maybe this was the man the good Lord sent to make her happy. When I looked at mama she didn't pay the man no mind.

How could I make her see that this was the man for her? This damn gift was sometimes a pain in the ass.

I finished eating and when I looked towards the man's table he was gone. I looked around and then out the window and he was getting into a nice car. He looked back at us and tipped his hat like the men did in the old movies Grammy and me watch. Then he got in his car and drove away.

Dammit, now I would never know how this man was supposed to fit into my mama's life. I still had this funny feeling that he is supposed to be with mama and now he's gone.

Damn this gift. "Damn" I heard myself say aloud. I hoped my mother didn't hear me, but no luck, the pop on the back of my head let me know that she heard me loud and clear.

"What did I tell you about cussing, young ladies aren't supposed to curse" mama said as she tapped me on the head again.

"I know mama, I'm sorry, I don't know where that came from" actually I knew exactly where that came from and if she wouldn't have popped me on the head there were a few more choice words that were about to fly. I can't help it, sometimes I like to freaking cuss, it calms my nerves.

We were headed toward the door and I still couldn't figure out this feeling. I didn't want to wait to see how this plays out. This gift gets me so impatient sometimes that I just want to cuss. So I let one fly "shit" I quickly ducked and looked in my mama's direction waiting for the hit that never came. My sister was laughing at me. Mama was having a serious discussion with the waitress.

The waitress explained to mama "Ma'am, the man in the back booth paid your bill and he left a healthy tip. He said that your meal was on him. He mentioned that you all looked like such a nice family that he wanted to pay for your meal." The waitress was smiling and crying at the same time.

I saw mama's eyes water, but she held it back and put on what Grammy calls her tough face, which ain't so tough and said "I didn't even get to thank him, that was so nice of him."

When we left the restaurant I was beaming, I knew there was something good about that man and I had the feeling we would see him again real soon, this gift thing is amazing.

My gift was in full effect "Hell yeah" I said a little too loud, my mama tried to pop me, but my sister was between the two of us and she got hit. "Sorry mama" I said with a smile "Sorry mama, I don't know where the hell that came from."

CHAPTER 3

LET ME DOWN EASY

During the walk home my mother's mood was very upbeat. She was telling us that there are still good people in the world and that no good deed goes unnoticed.

She was so happy that she suggested we stop by the playground so that Ty could play on the swing. Mama surprised us when she took a few passes on the swing and played with us on the teeter totter.

We ended our afternoon with a trip to our favorite place in the world, Cluster's. Cluster's was one of the few five and dimes stores left in the city that had a 1950's soda fountain. The shakes were awesome because the ice cream was handmade and they used gooey chocolate to make the shake really thick.

I was surprised that the man in the restaurant had made my mama so happy. I couldn't remember the last time my mama had ice cream. We raced to the end of our street. Mama won, I was in a close second. Ty was laughing so hard she could barely run.

This was turning into the perfect day.

"Mama, this was fun, we should do this all the time." Ty said in between giggles.

I added "I hope that one day we can thank the nice man. Maybe one day we could buy him lunch. Maybe you could make him dinner."

"Baby, what just happened is called a random act of kindness. The man was just being kind. Maybe we should pass on his act of kindness to someone else." mama's voice was soothing.

She was smiling as she played with my afro. She then knelt. I loved when she knelt down to my level and held my face in her hands; it made me feel like a little kid again. She must have known what I was thinking because she said "I don't care how grown you think you are, you will always be my baby girl, got it?"

"Got it, but mama, I'm damn near a teenager and almost five feet tall, one day soon I'm going to be six feet tall and pretty like you!"

Mama smiled and said "I believe you will."

As we get closer to our house I notice my daddy swinging on our porch swing. I had to think of something fast. I said "Dimmit, I left my purse at the restaurant, we have to go back"

Mama said "Sure, we can go back and get it, but please no more cursing."

"Thank you, mama. Can we go to Grammys' after we get my purse?" I said as we turned and headed back the way we came. Good thing she didn't see that monkey on our porch swing, now let's hope he didn't see us.

No such luck here he comes, damn. I looked over my shoulder and my old man is gaining on us, I told mama that we should race again and we sped up. Then my father starts to yell, "hey wait up for me, baby, where you all going in such a hurry"

I yell back "I lost my purse and we have to go back to find it, we'll see you some other time, run mama run" my mother stopped and grabs me by the shoulder. I try to keep running but she turns me around, then gives me that look that says give him a break, he is your father.

Ty yells to daddy and runs back to greet him.

A loud "shit fire" escapes my mouth. I look at my mother and say "sorry mama, I don't know where ...."

She cuts me off and says "that came from that filthy mouth of yours that I will wash out with soap later this evening, now go say hello to your father"

Great, way to go daddy dick head, you just screwed up what was a really fantastic family day.

CHAPTER 4

THE BIRDS AND THE BEES

Mama gave up sports after college. She was a basketball and track star. She now works at the high school and is assistant girls track coach. Her dream was to become a doctor. Grammy says that mama gave up her dreams to marry my father and travel from city to city as a basketball players' wife.

My father is Jay Norwell. You may have heard of him. He was a college basketball star and played during the sixties in the ABA. He played for the Washington Bullets, Indiana Pacers and Utah Stars.

My Uncle Len says daddy wasn't good enough to be a star in the pros. He said daddy had natural talent and that got him to the pros, but he didn't have enough smarts to keep him there. To be a success you need drive determination, hunger and a work ethic to be successful. If you're your daddy put into his game what he put into the women, drinking and gambling he could have had a decent career.

Grammy told me daddy is a loser from the word go. He was a no talent flake who can't keep it in his pants. He's an alcoholic who feels the world owes him.

My Grandmother tells me that I am a lot like my father. When she says that my eyes roll in circles they really do, I tell her with no disrespect that I may look like him, but we are nothing alike. If I am like him, Lord, please kill me where I stand.

My father and Ty were walking close to half a block ahead of me and mama. They are hand and hand headed back toward the house. Ty was talking a mile a minute and swinging daddy's arm. He gives her an occasional glance. I could hear my sister telling our father all about her day and all the fun she had. I could see that my father was only half interested. He was trying to match Ty's energy and failing miserably.

Mama and I could see that my father was smiling and nodding at Ty, but at the same time he kept glancing back at mama. When I heard Ty mention the nice man again, I saw my father's head snap as he turned and looked back at mama. He was not happy at all.

Wait a minute, was he jealous? He had some nerve, the womanizing little turd. I scrunched my face and stuck my tongue out at him. I couldn't help it; he had some nerve being jealous of my mother. The Bastard had another family across town.

My mother and I were walking slower now, I had my arm around her waist and she had her arm on my shoulder. We were having a good mother daughter moment.

"Do you still have feelings for him mama?" I asked. I looked up at my mother. She just looked straight ahead with a calm look.

Mama said "I don't know; I honestly don't know."

"Mama, if you don't love him, then why is you sad all the time?" I asked

"Well, when you marry someone you believe that no matter what happens, everything will work itself out and you will always be with that person. We are told that if you put your all into the marriage, you will receive the same in return. I feel like somewhere along the line, I failed. I put so much into our marriage, but got nothing in return. In the end not only did I lose my husband, I lost who I thought was my best friend. I lost a person that I thought I would always be with me, till death do we part. I know this is too much for you right now. Hopefully you will understand when you are older." Mama spoke in a quiet voice. It was almost like she was saying it more to herself than to me.

I shook her a little and said "well mama, he left his family; he's got another woman and other children. He left us, we didn't leave him. He hurt you, he makes you sad and you still cry for him. He has treated you bad and I'll always hate him for that."

"So, do you still love him?" I asked again. I didn't understand.

She replied "I love him, but I'm not in love with him."

What the hell does that mean? I heard that line on an old movie the other night. The boyfriend beat the girlfriend half to death. The police arrested the boyfriend. The lady was taken to a safe house. She was so scared. The social worker pulled up a seat and sat close to the woman. She took a deep breath and raised her voice and said to the woman "Doris, are you nuts? You know this has got to stop. Look at you. He's now beating your ass on a daily basis. You've been hospitalized five times. If you won't leave for yourself, leave for the kids' sake, dammit. I have to ask, Doris, why do you allow him to treat you so bad? You can't still love him, can you?"

"I love him, Bonnie, but I'm not in love with him. I just feel bad for him. He's really a good guy and all …..."

The social worker looked at her and said "honey look at yourself, he beat the crap out of you. If you go back to him he will kill you, maybe not today or tomorrow, but one day. You do realize that this is mental and physical abuse. How can you ever love him after what he is doing to you?"

She replied, I just do"

The social worker said "I will be sure to put that on your headstone, I loved him, but I wasn't in love with him and then he beat me to death!"

I looked up at mama and wondered how many times my father put his hands on her. I wondered why she didn't leave him earlier.

Ty and daddy were now in the house, me and mama had just made it to the porch. I stopped, not really feeling like going in the house.

I held my mother's hand and told her "mama, that man in there is killing you slowly and you are letting him do it. Here, sit down. Listen mama, you have loving children who need you! You have a career and a good life. C'mon Doris, don't let that man in there take that away from you dammit. Go out and find out who you are. Live your life Doris and be happy. If you don't want to do it for you, do it for the kids."

My mother paused, looked at me with a puzzled look. She paused again and slowly said "Doris, who in the world is Doris? Child, where are you getting all this grown up relationship talk from, you sound like a soap opera or one of them old movies your Grammy is always watching. My goodness, my mother is such a bad influence on you." Mama was now shaking her head.

Mama put her hands over her face like she was going to cry. Instead she started laughing. She was snorting and doubled over. Mama was out of control. She was laughing and crying at the same time. She reached for my hand and pulled me in close. "Are you getting all this talk from one of those old movies? Is that where this is coming from"

"Yes mama. That is what happened to Doris in the movie. Roger moved out of his house and left his wife and kids the same way daddy left us. Mama, you don't understand. Daddy ripped our family apart, just like Roger ripped his family apart. You are taking all the blame when the blame should be on him. He left you for another woman and made another family. He destroyed your love for him and now he is making you suffer. I'm sorry mama, but it's true and I feel it's time that you moved on and find true happiness."

Now mama was rolling. She wasn't just laughing, she was literally on the ground rolling around and laughing. She was screaming "Stop it, you're too funny, you're killing me and you're going to make me pee!"

I crossed my arms; I wasn't seeing anything funny about this. Here I was telling her that she needed to get her life together and she was laughing at me and acting childish. After a few minutes of watching her, I said "mama, get up, you are embarrassing me."

Mama finally settled down and sat up Indian style. She brushed the dirt off her clothes and picked grass out of her hair. I sat in her lap and she hugged me tight.

Mama said seriously "First thing tomorrow that TV comes out of your room and then we are going to have a long talk with that Grammy of yours."

"But mama doesn't Doris deserve to be happy? Once she thought about it, she moved on from her ex-husband and met Morris. Morris treats her like a queen. He makes her happy. Don't you want to be happy?"

Mama looked at me seriously and said "baby, as crazy as it sounds, there is a lot of truth to what they are saying." then she put her chin on the top of my head "you are such a smart little grown ass girl, I wouldn't know what to do without you, I love you baby."

"I love you too mama."

A brand new Buick Regal pulled up to the curb with daddy's new family inside. Me and mama waved hello to my half brother and sister. They waved back. Their mother was fidgeting with the stereo and didn't look our way.

"Mama, do you hate daddy's girlfriend? You know, for taking daddy from us." I asked

"No, baby, I don't hate her, it's not her fault. Let's just say I have a feeling that your father probably wasn't truly honest with her and we'll keep it at that."

Daddy came out and stood on the porch. He smiled and waved to his new family, then looked at my mother and said "I was looking for the deed to the house and couldn't find it anywhere in the study and where did you put the lock box with all my papers?"

Mama tensed up. She looked hard at my daddy. She said "You were in there rifling through my house looking for papers? I told you before; your name is no longer on the deed to this house. This is my house now. I got it in the divorce remember. Oh that's right you forfeited everything when you didn't make the court dates. Well, to save you time and effort in the future, anything of value is in my safe deposit box at the bank. I no longer trust you. Remember that the next time you decide to spend time with your daughter in my house. And to think, I thought you were in there spending quality time with your daughter."

Daddy was about to say something, but was cut off by the sound of the horn.

We looked toward the street as the horn blew again. We all looked at the car, then daddy looked at us. "I have to go, love you both" he patted me on the head, and then he tried to bend down and kiss me on the forehead.

"I am not a damn dog." I said while ducking so all he kissed was air. He could kiss my ass.

He looked at mama real nasty like and said "I hear you have a new boyfriend" then the horn blew again and daddy ran off to be with his new family, what a punk.

Me and mama sat hugged up for a while longer, not saying anything, just enjoying the quiet.

I looked up and said "mama when we see the man who bought us lunch, can we ask him over and make him a big dinner?"

"Baby, what makes you think we will ever see him again?"

"My gift mama, I just saw us all playing in the park and then going to Cluster's for shakes. He probably never had a Cluster's shake before. You were laughing, just like you were laughing today. He was laughing. He was looking at you the whole time like you were gravy and if he had a biscuit he would have just sopped you up"

Mama was laughing again and said "after we get rid of television and talk with Grammy, I'm going to talk to your uncle Len about telling you those tired old lines"

I helped mama up and then we went in the house to check on Ty and see what my father might have taken.

....

My brother Michael came through the back door and said "about time daddy's sorry ass left. I came around the corner and saw him sitting out there like a little porch monkey. He must have been sitting out there for hours. He was sitting out there for so long that I had to go down to the filling station to take a dump"

Ty started laughing as Michael grabbed a banana off the top of the refrigerator and put one hand in the air and the other under his arm and chased her around the kitchen making monkey sounds.

Mama asked Michael where he had been all day and Michael gave his patented answer "around, you know, here and there."

Mama hates when Michael doesn't tell her where he's been and Michael hates when she asks him questions. So to get everyone back in a good mood I shouted "Hey Mikey, mama has a boyfriend."

"That's good mama, I hope he makes you happy." Michael said

"He's not a boyfriend; we don't even know the man. He was just a nice man who bought us lunch at the diner. It was just a

24

good gesture." Mama answered and if I didn't know better I would say that she was blushing.

"Really now," Michael said rubbing his chin. "Young lady if you're going to start dating we are going to have to set some ground rules. First off you have to bring the young man around so we can meet him. I won't go for any of this sneaking around. Next I think we need to have that talk about them birds and them bees, just in case you forgot. Finally, when do you plan on telling Grammy about this man, I'm sure she has a few questions to ask your young man."

Mama got her own banana, peeled it and pointed it at Michael. She told him "Listen up little mister, you have one hot mama here. If a man wants to date me, he will have to come correct. I'm talking manners, respect, God fearing and he will treat me like the queen that I am. If he does that, then he will get a chance to meet your Grammy. After your Grammy interrogates him and lets him live, you all will get to meet him. I just don't bring anyone around my precious babies. And just in case you have forgotten, I schooled you on the birds and the bees."

Ty broke in and said "I want to learn about the birds and the bees"

Michael quickly said "birds sing and bees sting and that's all you need to know" mama and Michael high fived as they both took a seat at the table.

Ty sat on Michaels lap and I sat on mamas. Ty and I told Michael all about our day and told him we wished he would have come along. He told us he was hanging with the boys and that he might hang out with us next time.

We all continued to talk while mama made snacks. When mama finished, we all took a plate to the living room, got comfortable on the couch and watched TV. This turned out to be a great day.

CHAPTER 5

LET'S START OVER

Nicola Kimberly Norwell if you are not washed up dressed and at this table in ten minutes, I am going to come up there and hurt more than your little feelings.

I spoke to my reflection in the mirror. Mama is getting on my last good nerve and I am just not feeling her at all today. She better stay clear of Nicola Kimberly Norwell, because I am not taking shit off no one today. I hate when she says my full name and she knows it.

Ty was at the bathroom door giving me sass. "Nicola, mama said to hurry up. She also wanted to know, what's your major malfunction today, you cow"

"You said that, mama didn't say that, you little roach. Tell your mama I said I will be there when I get there and if she doesn't like it, she can bring her big bird, stretch Armstrong ass up here and get dealt with. Now get out my face before you get dealt with. And Nicola isn't my name anymore, it's Kim" I said rolling my eyes and then turning my back to Ty.

"Ooh, mama, Cola is cussing again" Ty yelled at the top of her voice. "She said you can kiss her butt" Ty looked back at me smiling as she stuck her tongue out.

"Mama, I never said that, Ty's lying on me." I yelled down the stairs. Then I looked at Ty then lowered my voice and said "You're just asking to get punched in the face."

A few months ago that threat would have made Ty back down and run to mama, but today she held her ground and said "I'll punch you in your face, bitch" and put up one fist and then mean mugged me, just like Mohamed Ali would do.

What was this, little sister standing up to big sister, oh no, we can't have this. I went to grab her and noticed that we were just about eye to eye. When did she get to my height? Then she pushed me backwards into bathroom, and put her finger in my face and said "I'm tired of your shit, I will kick your ass, and you hear me. Yeah, I can cuss too, but I choose not to because unlike you, I'm a lady. So you better stay out of my face," Then she turned and walked out of the bathroom.

I walked behind her and pushed her into my mother's bedroom. She then spun around, grabbed me and threw me onto my mother's bed. It was on now. We were wrestling and the next thing I knew; she was on top and my arms pinned. I told Ty if she didn't let me up, she was going to get her ass kicked. She put her face so close to mine that our noses touched and she said "Sorry big sister it ant going to happen, not today, not ever again, now say uncle"

"I ant saying uncle to you, get off me" I was pinned, but I wasn't giving up. I mustered up enough strength to roll her off me, but she was quick, she rolled me on my back again. Then we tussled and rolled right off the bed and hit the floor.

We were entwined, grunting and struggling. We never fought like this before and she never really put up much of a fight in the past. Ty had a look in her eyes that said she was going to win today.

I was tired, but determined not to let her win. "Big sister always beats little sister, that's sister law" I told her in my best Clint Eastwood voice.

Ty said "Sorry, big sister loses today." She began to tickle me.

I giggled "you better get off me."

Ty was giggling too; she said "who's your daddy, cow?"

I was laughing so hard now and yelling "you're my daddy, you cow."

Ty asked "what's my name?" as she stuck a finger in my ear

I said "Tyrone, your real name is Tyrone, mama and daddy wanted a boy and they named you Tyrone"

We were both laughing so hard that we couldn't move, so we just laid there on the floor. I looked at Ty and said "When did you get to be my size?"

Ty said "Seriously, haven't you noticed, I've been wearing your clothes for months. This is your sweater and these are your shoes."

"Wow, my little sister is growing up" was all I could say.

When we looked up, mama was standing over us.

She said "look what you did to my bed, when you two are done playing, make my bed, clean up and get you butts downstairs" then she left the room.

Ty asked "do you think she saw the whole fight?"

"She was probably laughing at us the whole time."

We helped each other up from the floor, and then started putting the bed back together. We were tucking in the corners when Ty looked over and said to me "that's the first time we fought for real, are we still cool"

"Yeah, were cool. I guess I had that coming, but just remember I'm your older sister and I will always be able to whoop your ass, got it" I said not really sure if that were true anymore.

Ty said "got it, but now you know who your daddy is. Her name is Tyreese Jessica Norwell and don't you forget it"

All I could do was smile. Today was a day of first, the first time my little sister stood up to me, the first time we fought and the first time that I heard her cuss. I was so proud of her.

Ty looked like a shorter version of my mother. Both had determined almond shaped eyes, deep dimples, a warm smile and perfect nose, they were gorgeous.

She really did look cute in my clothes and today she was wearing the hell out of my sweater.

CHAPTER 6

THANK GOD

When we made it to the breakfast table, we noticed that there were only place settings for three.

"Hey mama, where's Michael? Is he eating with us today?" I asked mama questions that I already knew the answers to. Lately my brother has been running the streets. Mama can't seem to get through to him anymore. He breaks curfew, he is disrespectful and most of the time when we try to talk him, it's like he isn't there. Grammy says "lights are on, but no one is home, that boy is a zombie"

Mama sat down at the table, moved a stray hair from Ty's face and we all joined hands to bless the food. Mama said "Your brother won't be joining us today, Kim, please say grace"

We lowered our heads. I prayed "Thank you, heavenly father for the food we are about to receive. Thank you for the nourishment and the goodness of this meal. Thank you for my mama, my sister and my brother, where ever he may be. Please make sure Michael is safe while he is running them streets. Please answer Grammy's prayer and make sure that boy is wearing a raincoat, even when it ain't raining because she's too young to be a great Grammy. Please keep Michael out of harm's way and finally please don't let him shit where he eats, those are my daddy's words, not mine. Amen"

When I opened my eyes my mama was looking at me with what my Grammy calls big saucer eyes. She said "thank you for blessing the food, but next time say your own words from your own heart. From this day forward you are never to repeat anything your Grammy, your uncle or your father say during prayer, are we clear?"

"Yes ma'am" I told my mother just as Michael walked through the back door.

Michael looked bad and smelled worse. He said a little "hey you all" and started for the stairs.

Mama called after him, "are you hungry? Go upstairs and wash up, then come down and get something to eat"

Michael called back over his shoulder "no mama, I'm good"

Mama looked really worried, I know on the one hand she was really pissed, but on the other hand she didn't want to have it out with him like she did a few days ago. Mama was yelling and Michael tried to walk away. I guess since he was high, he must have forgotten that mama knew karate and judo because next thing I knew Michael was on the floor and me and Ty were pulling on mama and begging her to stop punching him and let him off the floor. When Michael got up he yelled that he hated her and mama yelled that if he felt that way then he could go live with daddy.

We watched Michael make his way up the stairs.

I said "Mama, Michael must have shit where he ate at this morning because he stinks and his breath smells like monkey ass. Glad he didn't eat here."

Mama pointed and stared at me hard.

I stirred my cereal, looked in my bowl and said "just an observation"

CHAPTER 7

WHO HAS THE BEST AFRO

"Hello everybody, where's everybody at?" Grammy yelled from the front door entry way.

"Me and the kids are here in the kitchen, mother" mama yelled to Grammy from the as she continued to clean the rack on the stove that the peach cobbler spilled on to. I sat talking to Ty and Regina, arguing about which singing group had the best Afros, the Jackson Five, the Commodores, Shalamar, Earth wind and Fire or the Sylvers. They said the Jackson Five, I said Foster Sylvers.

"Hello my Children" Grammy said as she entered the kitchen. Mama stood gave Grammy a hug and a kiss on the cheek. Me and Ty sat at the table while Grammy came over and gave us a kiss on the cheek. Regina jumped up from her chair and ran around to Grammy. Regina pulled her close and gave her a great big hug and a kiss on the cheek. I noticed that Regina had grown an inch or two and was now the same height as Grammy.

Grammy was short and tiny, she looked almost frail, but any who knows her knew better. My Grammy was trough and would take on anybody.

Grammy was dressed very nice; she had on a pair of white Converse Chuck Taylors and white bell bottom jeans. The jean vest that she was wearing fit her snug and although she didn't have big bosoms, you could see a little cleavage. The silk, puffed sleeve shirt she wore was a flowery mix of orange and yellow. Her hair was styled in loose curls with a dash of gray on the temples that made her look distinguished. Her white roller skates were slung over her shoulder. If she wasn't my Grammy, I would think that she was mama's older sister. My Grammy looked good for her age. Tonight was skate night so Grammy wouldn't be staying long.

Grammy looked at Regina who was still hugging her. Regina looked at Grammy. Grammy held Regina at arm's length, looking at her like she was a lost puppy. Grammy said in between laughs, "Regina, you do know that I ain't your Grammy and you ain't my grandchild, right?" Regina nodded. "Good, now those two lazy asses over there who won't even get off their dead ass to show me love, they my grandchildren" Grammy put her hands on Regina's shoulders and said "Child, I have to ask, you are always over here, playing, eating and sleeping, do you even have a home? I mean, do you have parents, brothers and sisters? Do you have a Grammy of your own? Maybe someone who might notice that you ain't never there? I'm sure someone misses you? Maybe a dog, goldfish or someone misses you?"

Regina giggled and replied "I have a mama, a daddy, two older brothers and an older sister. My mama and Daddy live across the street, three houses down. You've met them a while ago. My brothers are ten and twelve years older than me and live in California. My sister is away at college, studying to be a doctor. I don't have anyone to play with at home, so I come over to play with my best friend Ty. My mama says that I can come over here and hang out as long as Ms. N doesn't mind and I don't become a bother."

Grammy said "OK child, just wanted to make sure aren't lost or a run away."

Regina giggled and said "Ty and Cola Kim are like sisters to me. So I see you as my Grammy too. My Grandparents live on an island, and I don't get to see them very often" Regina got a serious look on her face and asked Grammy "Can you be my Grammy too?"

Grammy was speechless. She pulled Regina in real close and quietly said "I would be honored to be your Grammy"

My Grammy has to be the coolest Grandmother ever. Her roller skates, rides a bike, drives a Mustang, dresses hip and has a great sense of humor.

Grammy lives four blocks away, so she is always close. Sometimes after school, if mama has to work late and Ty stays after school for an activity, I get to hang out with Grammy and have her all to myself. When Grammy knows that I am coming over, she'll usually make me a nice dinner and afterwards we play a game of cards while eating cookies and watching soap operas. Some weekends mama lets me and Ty stay with Grammy, we call it our girls weekend. We usually help Grammy around the house with chores and anything that she may need a hand with.

Grammy lives alone in a house that is half as big as ours. Her and my Grandfather was divorced long before I was born and she got the house. She has two big German Shepherds that mostly stay outside and a cat that always stays indoors. Her girlfriends come over and they play cards once or twice a week. Grammy has a couple of male friends that come calling often. Mr. Bob I think is her main man because he takes her on weekend trips to the casinos in Atlantic City and shopping in New York. Mr. Donald is who she calls her old buddy, takes her dancing and to fancy eating places around town. My history teacher, Mr. Franklin thinks that Grammy is a wonderful woman. You can bet that at least twice a day, he will ask me something about Grammy. He is a nice guy and all, but it seems just a little creepy to have your history teacher asking about your Grammy.

Grammy is always telling mama that she needs start dating. She says there are a lot of good men out there looking for a good woman. Mama tells Grammy that she has kids at home to raise and she is selective about the kind of men she wants to expose her children to.

Whenever Grammy talks about mama finding a good man, mama changes the subject by asking Grammy "when is my daddy coming to town."

My Granddaddy and mama's father is Big John Henry. He is a big man, very tall with big muscles. It is funny to see him and Grammy together because he is a foot and a half taller than her. Even though they are no longer married, you can see that they really care for each other. They are a really good looking couple too. If someone was to see Grammy and mama together, they would wonder where mama got her height, but when you see mama and her father together, you can quickly see. Mama and Granddaddy look a lot alike and act the same in many ways. My grandfather calls her his princess and tells everyone how proud he is to be her father. Unlike my piece of shit father who couldn't give a crap if I lived or died.

We get to see our Granddaddy mostly around the holidays. He takes us out riding in his big Cadillac and buys us things that mama and Grammy would never buy us. I wish he were around all of the time, he is a lot of fun. When Granddaddy comes to town Grammy doesn't see any of her man friends and Granddaddy always stays at her house. Grammy told me that they were best friends before they got married and will remain best friends until the day they die.

I asked mama why Grammy and Granddaddy aren't together. Mama laughed and said "Lord only knows.

When your uncles turned eighteen and moved away from home, your grandparents decided they needed to go out and do all of the things that they missed due to raising a family. So they divorced and started running around like kids, I guess they are both going through their second childhood. I pray that they figured out some day. Hopefully they will love each other and grow old together, because they really are a cute couple.

CHAPTER 8

PHANTOM LOVER

Ty had her arm around my neck and was whispering in my ear "Hey big sis, your knight in shining armor wants to meet you at the park, near the outdoor skating rink. I tried to get Rodney to come to the house, but he said that he would be more comfortable if you all just met at the playground", I guess she didn't want mama to hear. Regina is Ty's best friend and was standing in the corner giggling; she was always giggling or laughing at something.

I heard myself say "let's go" in a voice that sounded a lot calmer than I felt. My stomach was doing flip flops and my hands were sweating. I was surprised that I was able to keep up with Regina and Ty as we walked. When we got to the corner, Regina and Ty stopped and told me that Rodney would be by the skating rink a little later. "How will I know him, remember, I have never seen him" Now I was really nervous and I think I might have croaked instead of actually speaking.

Regina started giggling and said "Don't worry when he sees you, he will come over to you. Just be yourself and try not to cuss or roll your eyes or be sarcastic or mean or hit him. All I am saying is give him a chance. Give me that damn gum; you are popping it like a crazy mad cow. Are you nervous? Here's some licorice, if your need something to chew on at least it won't make too much noise. Remember that he's just a boy and you talk to boys all the time. He's a lot taller than you, so you may want to sit down, so you are eye to eye.

Regina was firing questions at me a mile a minute. I didn't have a chance to answer any of her questions. When she finally paused to take a breath, I asked her "wait, what do either of you know about boys?"

"A lot more than you do" they said in tandem. "If he wants a kiss are you going to let him kiss you?" Regina and Ty were staring at me so hard that I barely heard the part about a kiss.

"My first kiss, now that would be nice. This was something that I didn't think about. Should I change my name? Cola Price, no Kim Price, Mrs. Rodney Price, yeah I like that. This is my husband Rodney and our three kids, no four kids. Honey would you like to live in the country or New York City" I must have said this out loud because Regina actually stopped laughing and Ty said I want to be your bridesmaid and they were gushing.

What the hell? …..... "What if he is a geek with buck teeth and huge glasses? What if I don't like him or he stinks or worse or his breath was a nasty green cloud of funk" I said, totally changing gears. Regina laughed and said, trust me, I would marry him in a minute.

Now I was thinking that this is all a mistake. How could I let Ty talk me into this? I was really not feeling this and all I wanted to do was go home, lie in the bed and put my head under the pillow. But I couldn't because somehow I was moving in the direction of the skating rink. Ty and Regina were pushing me and still giving me advice. Regina was now laughing really loud and it was pissing me off.

By the time I realized I wasn't moving I was ten feet from the rink. Ty and Regina had abandoned me and it was too late to run for the cover of the trees. I looked straight ahead. I didn't see any geeks coming my way, no ten-foot-tall handsome guys checking me out, no pigpen looking boy in a funk cloud approaching, I was all alone with no one in sight. "I've been stood up! It was all a joke, ain't this a bitch. Ty and Regina are getting a beating" I said to myself. As I turned to leave I saw a boy headed my way and yes, he was tall, about a head taller than me. He had a Michael Jackson Afro, with a dark chocolate complexion and the whitest teeth I have ever seen; he was fine, damn fine.

"What's happening, Kim, I'm Rodney, when I first saw you, I knew I had to meet you, hi" he said it all very fast and in a not too soft, not too hard, but very nice voice. I can't really tell you what happened, but we hit it off right away. I guess we both must have been pretty nervous because we finished off the whole pack of licorice and the pack of bubble yum he had in his pocket.

I think I told him everything thing I could think of about myself by the time the sun started going behind the trees. I even told him that I knew his cousin and punched him in the face because he called me evil. He liked that I didn't take crap off his cousin. As it turns out Rodney is thirteen, only one year older than me. He told me all about himself and how he was good in all sports. He was very smart and the total opposite of his cousin Johnny. He told me that math just seemed to come easy to him, so he would like to be an accountant, like his father. He also told me that his mother passed away a few years ago and he missed her a lot. I wanted to cry and hold him, but I just watched as he looked down at his shoes.

I think I floated on air all the way back to the house with Rodney walking beside me instep. This was awesome and I never had a feeling like this before. When we reached the porch Regina and Ty were swinging on the porch swing, laughing and mama was leaning against the pillar. Mama looked very peaceful and was smiling when we came close. Mama spoke first "Young man, you do realize that this is my daughter that you are walking with. What is your name, how old are you and who are your parents" Mama said this in a nice soothing tone, so I knew that she wasn't pissed?

Rodney coughed then said "My name is Rodney Price ma'am, I'm thirteen and I go to school with Ty. My father is Stewart Price and my mama was Lavonia, she passed two years ago"

"Rodney, I know who you are" Mama smiled. I know your father and I was best friends with your mother. Mama started. I used to bring my children over to your house when you all were very young. You and Cola used to play together. The two of you would play all day and cry it was time for us to go home. I guess the two of you were too young to remember each other. It's nice that you two have found each other"

Mama leaned forward and the smile left her face, she then went into lawyer mode on his ass. The next 10 minutes were grueling, she threw a barrage of questions at him that he handled like a pro. His answers were short, sweet and to the point, no stuttering and no hesitation, it looked like he may live. I was so proud of him and even though we just met, he had my respect. I think I like him. Then he said to my mother in a very respectful manner, "Mrs. N. excuse me ma'am, but I have to get home before the street lights come on"

Mama smiled and said "go on and get home, tell your father hello for me. You can come back tomorrow afternoon; I have a few more questions I'd like to ask you. Cola, tell our little friend goodbye. Regina and Ty stop laughing, Ty get your butt in the house and Regina I think you better get a move on before the street lights catch you and your mama tans your hide" Mama stood right there on the porch, didn't move an inch. So I said goodbye to Rodney and he said goodbye back. He shook my hand, turned and ran down the street. I was thinking that if mama wasn't standing on the porch, that this evening would have been the day that I got my first kiss.

CHAPTER 9

BE MY GIRL

Mama finally got us out of the house and onto the porch. "Shotgun" I called and ran to the passenger side of the car. At the car, Mama quietly asked "why don't the two of you sit in the back today, mama has a few things on her mind" This was odd, usually who ever made it to the passenger side door first got to sit in the front seat.

"But Mama I called shotgun and I made it to the car first" I said in protest.

"Today, I think you and your sister should sit in the back and talk to each other, give me some time to think and drive in peace. Anyway whoever sits in the front always wants to turn around in their seat and talk to the one in the back. Today why don't the two of you sit together?"

Mama had a good point; I always twisted in the front seat to talk to Ty in the back seat. Since our big fight earlier, Ty and I have been inseparable. We made all of the beds together, had a coloring contest during breakfast, ate the same cereal and helped mama with the dishes. Before today this would have never happened.

We agreed and sat in the back seat. The moment Ty shut the door we started talking about school, boys and the latest gossip.

Ty looked at me, smiled slyly like she had a secret to tell me, then turned away like she was looking out the window, except her head was pointed in that direction and her eyes were cut toward me. Something was on her mind and I wanted to know. "What are you grinning about ?" I asked full of curiosity.

"You have a secret admirer that goes to my school, I hear he really likes you" Ty said to me while still looking out of the window. "You may have heard of him; his name is Rodney Price?"

I started thinking, then shook my head "no, I don't think I heard of Rodney, but I do know Johnny Price. He has like five or six brothers and one brother is just as bad as the other. I overheard a teacher say the other day that all those little Price bastards are on the fast track to jail or hell" I looked up in time to see mama's eyes in the rear view mirror, giving me a glare that said watch the cussing. I rolled my eyes, whatever and looked back to Ty and asked "you're not trying to hook me up with one of them little bastards are you" This got mama's attention and the slap on the knee from her got my attention. Damn she was quick with them long ass arms, I didn't see that one coming. I wanted to tell her two hands on the wheel at all times, but that could get me killed.

Ty continued "Those are his cousins, Rodney isn't like them, he is kind of a quiet kid, no real friends and a nerd, but a nice enough boy. Regina is in most of his classes, she said he saw you last week when you brought me my lunch money and he was staring and drooling all over the window"

"That doesn't mean he likes me. He was probably just enjoying the view, what boy can't keep his eyes off all this beauty. At my school I got all the boys drooling" I said with confidence. Truth was no boys ever looked my way. If I wasn't so good in basketball and baseball, I doubt any of the boys would ever talk to me.

"Anyway" Ty said dismissing me with a hand wave "Rodney asked Regina your name and what school you went to. She told him your name and that you were my sister. Today he handed me a note to give to you" Ty turned and looked out the window again.

It still wasn't registering that a boy actually liked me and asked about me. A boy from Ty's school, that meant he was smart. At Ty's school you had to pass a test and be handpicked to get in. This is too cool I thought to myself. So far I had two crushes in my life. One was on a boy they called dirty Red. Red was always funky. The kids said that he smelled like Campbell vegetable soup. He was cute as hell with his big red Afro. People teased him a lot because his teeth went every which way and his breath came out in a green funk fog. No way could I be seen with mush mouth, so I just kept my crush on him to myself.

Johnny Price was my other crush; he doesn't know that I used to like him. He was and still is a good looking kid. Whatever I could dish out, he could take and we would always give each other a hard time. One day he called me evil and raised his hand like he would hit me. My daddy is always calling me evil. I was so pissed that I snapped. I must have hit him five times in the face before he hit the ground. He did apologize and I forgave him. We even talk from time to time. But let me tell you, I may have said I forgave him, but I will never forget, oh no. Next time I won't just punch his lights out, but I will kick the living shit out of him if he ever call me evil .... oops, must have been having a flashback.

"Hey knot head, do you want the letter or not" Ty was waving a piece of paper in front of my face. I couldn't talk and all I was thinking was that a boy liked me. My insides turned to mush, I wanted to scream at the top of my lungs and I wanted to snatch the letter from her hand and tear it open. Instead I looked at Ty coolly and said, "Yeah, I guess I'll see what the boy has to say" Mama smiled at me in the rear view mirror, I guess Ty must have told her all about Rodney.

I could see mama's eyes in the mirror and the little wrinkles around them told me she was smiling. I smiled back and gave her a little wave. I looked at the paper which was folded nice and neat to look like a real envelope. I slowly unfolded it and it popped into a type of pyramid and written in the neatest writing I have ever seen, it had numbers one through four on each outside panel, I picked four. I opened and closed it four times. Inside it said pick a color, I chose green and lifted the panel. It read, "I saw you yesterday and I think you are the cutest girl I have ever seen, would you be my friend" then there were two boxes, one said yes and the other said no.

I looked over and Ty was waving a pen in front of my face and she was saying "you know you ain't got no friends, just go ahead and mark yes and I'll give it back to him tomorrow after homeroom" I took the pen and filled in the yes block. I then handed the pen and paper back to Ty and above yes she wrote in big capital letters the words 'HELL YES' and stuffed the note in her back pack.

I must have still been reeling with delight, because Ty reached over and squeezed my cheeks until I had duck lips and whispered "he seems like a nice guy, don't screw this up. He may be the best and only friend you may ever have, besides me. The only reason that I put up with your shit is because mama pays me too"

"Oh, now you cussing," I gave Ty a shocked look. "Mama did you hear Ty back here cussin'" Mama looked in the rear view mirror and put a hand to her ear "what was that honey, it's hard for me to hear while I'm paying attention to the road"

Ty looked at me and stuck her tongue out and said "I guess you didn't see that one coming"

....

We rode the rest of the way to the store in silence. I tried to remember if I ever knew anyone that I called a friend, or someone that called me friend. The only person I could come up with was a white girl named Alice. Alice's family lived next door to us until I was in the fifth grade. Alice and I did everything together and we were inseparable. She was a tough little girl and a tom boy just like me.

One day we were walking home from school and out of the blue, Alice started to cry. She said her parents were selling their house and they were moving to a place called the suburbs at the end of the school year. She told me her father said it would be the best for her family. He told her that the neighborhood is changing and the colored are moving in. He said it's best they leave while they can get a good price for the house, before property values dive. He also told her she would love the suburbs. It is a pure neighborhood and she would have a great big yard with kids to play with that were just like her. She told me she was scared and didn't want to leave her room and that I was her only friend. Alice also told me that when she asked her father if my family could move next door to them, her father laughed and said "no honey your friend and her family are the ones we are moving away from"

I wasn't sure what this was all about. We were just alike and we played all of the time, couldn't her father see that. Our mothers have been friends forever. I'm sure mama wouldn't mind living someplace nice, with a big yard right next door to Alice's family.

When we got to the house mama and Alice's' mother were standing at the fence talking like they did every day. Alice and I gave them hugs, then went to the back of the house and took turns pushing each other in the big tire swing in her family's backyard. I asked her about the suburbs and she said it had lots of grass, no trees and dirt. There are no stores on the corner and not many kids running around. She told me it was boring. She couldn't understand why people would want to live there.

That afternoon when Grammy came over, I told her about Alice moving to the suburbs and all the things Alice's father said. I asked if we could move to the suburbs to be next to Alice, because she would be all alone with no friends.

Grammy explained to me that Alice was white and I was colored. Her father is a bigot, like Archie Bunker on the TV show all in the family. He believes that white folk are better than colored and he don't want to be nowhere near us. Honey when white folks start talking about the open spaces, property values and the suburbs, it's called "white flight" It's just another way of saying that they are running away from us colored folks to be with their own kind. Now don't let nothing Alice's father said come between you and Alice. You and that girl have been friends since forever. Color never mattered to the both of you and don't let it come between you now.

Grammy said all the white people were moving to the suburbs to get away from colored people. She said she was glad to see them go. Let us colored folk have something that we can call our own.

....

A few days after we finished the fifth grade, Alice moved away. I spent most of the summer on the back porch looking at the big tire swing, missing Alice.

When school started in September, I was in the sixth grade. The school had changed, a lot. We now had a black principal and a few more black teachers. I looked around for familiar faces from the year before, maybe I could meet up with someone and we could be friends. A lot of the new kids were from the projects or other black neighborhoods and already knew each other.

Some of the new girls were much bigger than and not as friendly as the girls that were already going to my school. Everyone seemed to get along with not much hassle. This was a big change for me; last year there were only four black kids in my class of twenty, now I count twelve.

......

Hopefully Rodney Price and I hit it off as friends from the start, because it would be nice to have a good friend again.

CHAPTER 10

BABY, I'VE BEEN MISSING YOU

It was Sunday afternoon, we just came from church, and we were in the kitchen talking about nothing when the doorbell rang. Mama asked me to get the door since I was closest. I looked out the window and walked back to the kitchen. "Who was at the door Cola?" mama asked. "My biological" mama looked at me, then looked behind me and asked, "well, where is he?" I looked around and said "Oh, I don't know, I guess he'll be back later"

The doorbell rang, then came a pounding on the door. I looked toward the living room and said "damn, is that man back already and why is he pounding on the door like he the police?" mama smiled, rolled her eyes and said, "girl, go let your daddy in and quit acting silly. Biological, you need to stop"

I opened the door and stood behind it like I always did. He entered the foyer and said his usual greeting "hey baby girl, does daddy get a hug?" I gave him my craziest, have you lost your mind look and then answered "Sorry daddy, I can't hug you, I'm fighting a cold and wouldn't want to pass it on to you and your new family, mama and Ty are in the kitchen, go on in" He looked pissed and said "you always got something wrong with you, maybe you should see a doctor" I put my hands over my mouth and coughed then told him "I did see a doctor and he said that I will feel better soon" I gave a weak smile and muttered under my breath "just as soon as you leave, roach"

He walked over to mama and leaned down and gave her a big hug and a kiss on the head as if they were still married, ugh. Flaky bastard, one minute he treats her like shit, next he's all up on her. How could she stand the touch of this man who always reeks of stank beer and cigarettes. He put on a few pounds and if I'm counting correctly he is a few teeth short of the thirty-two the good lord gave us. At the rate he's losing teeth he'll be a jack-o-lantern by Halloween.

Mama was sitting there tolerating his lame ass and laughing at his corny sex jokes. He seemed to be coming around more often lately, bearing gifts and handing out dollars to my sister. When he gave my sister money she would try to give me half. I always told her that I didn't want his money. She would then tell me that once he gave the money to her, it was hers to do what she wanted with it and she wanted to share it with me. Truth be told, I really did need the money, but my darn pride just wouldn't let me take it.

Mama asked daddy, "so what are you going to do about Michael, if you are here to talk to him, you are two days to late. You told me that you would be here Friday after school to talk with him?"

He started with the "aw baby......." excuse, but mama cut him short.

:

"Look, you promised to be more of a part of his life and you aren't doing much to help raise him. You need to remember that Michael was here first and he is your first child. You were never there for him as a child because of traveling and playing basketball. When he was a young teen you were off with your new family and now that he is almost eighteen you may be too late to get through to him. Look, the neighborhood is changing and the streets are getting harder and maybe a little fatherly advice will help him get through high school" Mama was damn near pleading with the man and he was playing her off and that really pissed me off.

Now look baby, he is going to be just fine. He's my son and as a Nowell we always bounce back. Hell, he is just going through a phase, I did it as a kid and he will go through it too"

Mama stood back and put her hand on her hip and raised one eyebrow. "Are you high on stupid or what, your son leaves on Friday and some weekends we are lucky to see him before Sunday morning. How about if I send him your way and you take care of him while he is going through this phase; I have had enough of his attitude. What you need to do is man up and save your son from the streets. If you didn't come by to talk to your son, why the hell are you here"

"Aw, well, um baby, I figured that since I was in the neighborhood, that I would check up on my family" Daddy was saying this while looking at the floor.

"Don't baby me and your new family is on the other side of town, so you best get over there for dinner, because you ain't mooching any meal here today." Mama was pointing a wooden spoon at him with a glob of mashed potato on the end. When she flicked the spoon some of the potato got in daddy's hair.

Daddy didn't notice and mama looked and smiled at me. I bet she did that on purpose.

Daddy started to speak again and mama went off on him, I think she called him everything, but a child of God. I was tired of this man and decided to get Ty and we could head outside.

I looked around the kitchen and didn't see Ty. This was odd; usually Ty was right there sitting on his lap while he and mama talked. He would tell her that she was his favorite girl and she would giggle and stick her tongue out at me.

I went to the back door walking between mama and daddy, not excusing myself. As I was going out the back door, I heard my father say "she needs to learn some manners, an excuse me would suffice" I let the door slam and mumbled "excuse you punk, I believe this is my house" He opened the door and yelled "what did you say young lady, you know you're not to old to get a whipping"

I was thinking, the last thing you want me to do is tell my brother Michael that you threatened to put your hands on me. He'll jack you up like the last time he heard you threaten me or worse yet, he'll cut your throat with the straight razor that he carries around.

I went to the picnic table next to the garage and took a seat next to my sister on the bench. "Girl what's up with you, why ain't you in there talking with your old man, keeping him out of everyone's hair?"

Ty ran her hand through her hair and said "I don't know, I'm just not sure if I like him anymore. I don't like when he yells at you and Michael and I hate the way he treats mama. It just isn't right"

I rubbed her back and told her "Ty, listen to me you have the father daughter thing going and it works for you. You need to have that relationship and be the good little girl your daddy wants you to be. Me on the other hand I don't need him for a daddy. He had his chance to be a father and blew it. Me and your old man have an understanding relationship, he understands that I hate him and I understand that I hate him and that's the relationship we will always have, a hate, hate relationship, end of story. I know hate is a harsh word, but until I find one that is harsher, I will stick with hate"

Ty looked at me, nodded her head up and down and said "mama was right, you do sound just like an old movie. Where do you get this crap?"

I laughed and told her "I got that from Grammy; she said that about our grandpa, she called him a waste of skin and space, breathing my good air"

....

Meanwhile back in the kitchen:

Ty and I had listened to mama and daddy from the back steps, we heard my father say "Look, my name is still on this house and I say that we need to sell this house and make a lot of cash, before the neighborhood becomes too black"

Mama was furious and lit into him. "Sell my house? Have you lost my mind? You have some gall coming in here asking me to leave my home. Where would I go or where would I live? I have a son and two daughters and this is the only home my children know. That's right, I said my children. Not only have you not been here for them, but you barely pay the measly support that is due me. The only reason your name is partially on the lease is because in this day and age, it is hard for a black woman to get a loan and own her own home.

Mama's leaned on the counter and crossed her arms "Kim told me last time you were here that she overheard you on the phone telling someone that as soon as you find the deed, you would be ready to sell this house"

Daddy had his hands in the air pleading "What, no, Tanya, please, you know that Kim can't stand me and she would say just about anything to drive me away. Who are you going to believe, me or a lying evil little twelve-year-old bitch. Your mother probably put her up to saying that"

Mama spun on daddy fast and pointed her finger dead in his face "That is your daughter that you are talking about and you have no right calling her something so dreadful, you bastard. Kim dislikes you as it is and with good reason, you have ignored her since the divorce. She is a good kid and if you treated her half way decent you would see this. I know she wouldn't make something up like that out of spite. Tell the truth and shame the devil. You are trying to sell my house out from underneath me aren't you? Yeah I know you are, you don't have to say a word. This is the cruelest thing that you have ever tried to do to me and I won't stand for this, I will fight you tooth and nail for this house until the very end.

Daddy's voice softened, he knew he screwed up royally "Tanya, this is 1973; you need to sell this house right now while white folk are still in this neighborhood. White people are moving away from here every day and selling their homes to black folk for good money. Those Negros are moving up here from the west end and the projects. With the highway going through the west end the city is buying up black folk houses. Them niggers are getting paid and moving on up, they are buying houses in this neighborhood and paying top dollar. Tanya, baby, I can get double what I paid for this house ten years ago, but we have to get the house on the market soon.

Mama said in a low but stern voice "I ain't selling my damn house. Let the black folks come from all over the city, I don't care, they are my people and if you hadn't noticed, you were once one of them. Remember when we moved here from the west end, we were the first blacks on this block. Hell, we were the first colored folks in this area. Did you forget how long it took the whites to accept us? The only reason that they didn't burn this house to the ground with us in it was because at the time you were playing pro basketball. Little did they know that you were running around screwing their wives and daughters every chance you got.

Mama got really loud now "You know what, you need to get the hell out of my house and never step in here again. I will not deny you visitation of your kids, but you won't be doing it in my house. If today wasn't Sunday, I would tell you what I am really thinking of you and trust me it wouldn't be nice. Go back to your new white wife and your half white kids in your lily white suburban neighborhood and leave me and the rest of the niggers alone. Oh yeah, I forgot it's her house and not yours and you have no say in what goes on in her house. You are pathetic, trying to run my household because you don't have a say in what goes on in that white lady's house on the other side of town. You ain't any kind of a man, you ain't shit. Get out of my kitchen before I call the police"

Daddy kicked the table and stormed out of the front door.

If Ty wouldn't have blocked me from going in the kitchen, I would have run to the carving board, grabbed the biggest knife I could find and sliced him into a thousand small pieces and buried him in the backyard, just beep enough so the dogs couldn't get to him or sliced his throat from ear to ear, giving him a second smile or better yet killed him and dissolve him in an acid bath.

Okay, maybe Grammy is a bad influence and just maybe I do watch too many old movies. But at this moment I would have gutted him like a fish, because no one calls me an evil bitch and lives to tell about it.

CHAPTER 11

YOU WERE MEANT FOR ME

It took us the rest of the night to calm mama down. My daddy could get her so worked up sometimes. It was like he had no control in his other house and would come by here just to see if he could get mama all riled up. I bet his new wife doesn't take one bit of his crap.

We were in the living room; mama was sitting on the love seat, me and Ty sitting next to her. Mama stroked our hair and we all stared at the television that wasn't on. So much for a happy Sunday afternoon. The knock on the door startled all of us, no one moved. Mama asked Ty to get the door, but I got up too, just in case daddy came back. We looked out the window before answering and saw Rodney.

Rodney saw us in the window, smiled and waved. I smiled big and waved back. Ty opened the door and invited him in. Rodney had the biggest smile on his face; in fact his smile was so big that it lit up the room. "Hello everyone" he said when he entered the room. My mama stood up and smiled. She straightened her dress and said "how are you doing today, young man?" Rodney continued to smile and said "I'm doing great and how are you today?" mama smiled and said "I'm doing better now; actually, I'm doing good and thank you"

Regina stuck her head in the door as we were finishing our greetings. She stepped in the house and said "Hey, hey, hey, what's happening?" Regina loved to hug and she hugged everyone, no one was a stranger. She made her rounds, hugging mama, Ty and then me. When she got to Rodney, she said "what up brother, give it up, bring it in, when you in this house you show love" and she gave him a big hug. She caught him off guard, if he wasn't so dark, he would have blushed.

Regina, being her crazy self said to mama "Hey Ms. N, my mama didn't feel like cooking today and said it would be alright if I ate over here. Uh, what's up, where's the smell goods, the chow, the grub you know, Sunday dinner. I know you all cooked something, you cook every Sunday and I eat here every Sunday remember" She sniffed the air again and said I ain't smelling no food, is the stove broke?"

Ty said "no Regina, daddy came by with drama and we never got a chance to finish cooking" Regina howled "Oh lawd, I'm gonna starve. I had my stomach all set for me some Ms. N's good cooking?"

We all laughed and Ty said "you're such a drama queen. Mama what are we gonna do for dinner, can we at the Diner, please" Mama looked at all of us and said "tell you what, we can get food at the diner and take it to the park. Rodney, would you like to join us?"

Rodney's eyes were as big as saucers and he said, "Yes ma'am, I love the diner and we hardly ever go there. I'll have to call my father to ask" Mama told him "I'll call your father and invite him along; we have some catching up to do. I guess since we'll be seeing a lot more of you, we had better get reacquainted. Mama told us to go outside and she would get us when she was ready to go.

. . . .

The Diner was six blocks and a good fifteen-minute walk from the house. It seemed like we made the walk in no time. We ordered the Sunday dinner basket and all the fixing's. Mama ordered a big jug of root beer to drink and sweet potato pie for dessert.

"Dang, Ms. N, I am glad you got all this food because I am starving" Regina said rubbing her hands together "What are the rest of you all going to eat?"

Mama said "girl, this isn't all for you, I invited your parents and Rodney's father to join us"

Rodney smiled at mama and said "Cool, I mean thank you for inviting my father, he hasn't really been out of the house for quite some time"

Regina, Ty and I looked at each other wide eyed thinking the same thing, what was up with mama and Rodney's father?

Mama must have sensed what we were thinking because on the way to the park, she told us about how she grew up with Rodney's parents and about Rodney's mother being her best friend.

Mama spoke of her childhood best friend from time to time and how she had passed away from cancer, but never really said much else. I have noticed that since Rodney has been coming around that mama hasn't been in her usual funk. Used to be that daddy would act up like he did this morning and mama would be in a funk for days. Michael wouldn't hang around the family or not come home, mama would mope. Today, Rodney shows up and here we are headed to the park for Sunday dinner. Maybe Rodney has the same effect on mama that he has on me. I like being around him and he makes me want to get out and have a good time.

Mama just has to realize, that this is my man and am not going to be no sharing, she will have to get her own man.

CHAPTER 12

YOU'RE GONNA NEED ME

Cola was lying in bed; she looked toward the window, still dark outside. She looked toward the hallway; the glow from the night light in the bathroom illuminated the second floor hallway with a warm glow. She didn't have a clock in her room. She had no idea of what time it was, so she laid very staring at the ceiling. She watched a streak of light that shown from the gap in the curtain. She figured the light must be coming from Mrs. Moody's porch light or the street lamp on the corner. Either way the streak of light reminded her of something from Star Trek.

Cola laid there for what felt like an eternity, but in reality must have been an hour. A million thoughts raced through her mind. Today she turns thirteen. Should she ask for a dog or a cat? Definitely a dog, but then she would have to clean up dog poop, no dog. A hamster or a fish would be nice, no poop to clean up. No, she didn't really want an animal at all; she wasn't an animal lover like Ty. They had a chocolate cake with white icing and sprinkles or yellow cake with chocolate icing? Ooh, yellow cake. Blueberry waffles or banana pecan pancakes for breakfast. Definitely pancakes because she had waffles last year. Dinner would be her favorite turkey and any side dishes mama decided to make.

Today was her big day, she turns thirteen. In her mind she is not just a teenager, but a grown woman. The world is now hers and things are going to change. Queen Cola, no Queen Kim. Today is the day she changes her name. From this day forward she will only answer to Kim. She will tell her mother first thing in the morning, well after she tells Ty, because Ty gets pissed if she is not the first to know everything. Then she'll have to let Rodney know, but he has always called her Kim, so no big deal. Then she will tell Grandma Nicole, the one she was named after. Of course Grandma Nicole will tell her what a wonderful name her God given name Nicole is and how she carried that name all her life. Cola has heard it all before. This time she will stand up to her grandmother and tell her how Nicole is an old ladies name and if she ain't noticed, she is a teenager, not any old lady. Kim smiles as she imagines the look on her grandmothers face when she tells her.

Finally, she will tell her daddy. She figures she'll say something like dad, from this day forward I would like to be called Kim. No more Cola or Cola bear, I'm not your little one or little sport or any other freaking corny ass nickname you call me, please, just call me Kim. She chuckles at the thought of him getting all pissy and saying "Girl, this was my mama's name and the name God gave you" she heard this so many times before, but this time will be different, she will stand her ground. She will tell him "screw you bastard, I'm thirteen years old, yaw dig. You're the one who screwed up my name when I was born. I was supposed to be Kim and today I am. By the way, if you call me evil again, I'll kill yaw!

This was going to be her best birthday ever.

CHAPTER 13

ANOTHER KISS TO GO

Peterson James Mitchell hasn't been to his hometown of Cincinnati, Ohio in over twenty-five years. Peterson signed up for the Coast Guard in January of his senior year. He received his high school diploma June fifth and shipped out to Cape May, New Jersey five days later for basic training. Peterson and his best friend Roger had joined the Coast Guard with plans of traveling the coast, flying helicopters and saving lives, just like the recruiter had promised them. Well for Peterson his dream came true, he traveled extensively on both coast, the Gulf of Mexico and Alaska. His best friend Roger however grew tired of the sea and the job of helicopter mechanic and left the Coast Guard after his first tour.

Peterson loved the Coast Guard and he truly enjoyed the travel. During his stint in the Coast Guard he received a college degree and was a decorated helicopter pilot. Upon his retirement after twenty-four year of service, he settled in Seattle, Washington, the city where he was stationed the majority of his career. Life in Seattle was good. Each year he would fly his parents and siblings out for a three-week visit. His parents were die hard Cincinnatians and although they enjoyed their visits to Seattle, it was not enough to leave their home in Cincinnati. Each year when their visit ended and they headed back to their home in the Midwest, Peterson felt a piece of his heart go back to Cincinnati with them. He knew that the family was getting older and the yearly visits were taking its toll. He could not expect them to visit him all the time, the road went both ways and it was time that he made his way back to Cincinnati to be back with the family.

Although Peterson was born and raised in Cincinnati, he always felt that the city was very conservative, stuffy and a little slow. He had traveled to a lot of places around the world. He always felt that he was having fun, living life. He loved to explore new places, sample all they had to offer and party like the natives. He also enjoyed the women who were so beautiful and exotic. But he he knew something was missing.

During his parents' last visit, Peterson noticed that his father would touch his mother's hand in a way that was so gentle, almost like if he pressed too hard she would break. When they walked it was as though they were gliding effortlessly across a dance floor. He noticed if they were ever in different rooms, his father would always look in on his mother to see that she was doing alright and his mother would do the same for his father. Even though his parents were just an older version of the fun loving couple they were raising him, they seemed to be bonded, almost joined at the hip. His mother still chuckled at his father's corny jokes and his father still listened intensely to what his mother had to say. Each accepted the other as they were, never trying to change one another, what they had was so beautiful.

Peterson had never been in a long lasting or meaningful relationship. He never really thought much about soul mates and true love. Actually he thought soul mates were something people called each other to say to the world that "hey we have something you will never have, we are special, we are soul mates" ….... bullshit. Peterson also had a belief that the greeting cards in the drug stores were there to sell people on the ideal of love. Give that special person a card and they will love you ……. yeah right. Peterson believed people fall in love with the idea of love.

Looking at his parents and seeing love first hand, he now understood why people were trying to find that one person to love. Someone to accept you as you are and in return you accept them as they are no questions, no doubts.

Peterson was standing on his deck watching as his parents slowly walked the beach hand in hand. They wanted to take a final stroll on the beach before they headed back to the chilly fall temperatures of Cincinnati. His mother wore his father's sweater, because she always had a chill. Peterson smiled at the thought of his father always carrying that old cardigan sweater. Then it dawned on him that his father wasn't carrying it for himself, he carried it for his mother, and he never saw his father actually wear the darn thing. His parents were enjoying the beach, but most of all they were enjoying each other. Peterson got his camera from the den and took a picture. He would later blow it up and hang it by the sliding glass door that leads to the beach.

At the airport while they were saying their goodbyes, Peterson hugged his mother and held on tight. Then he walked to his father and gave him a strong handshake, then a nice long hug. This was the ritual he always did when his parents left him, except this time, he told his parents that he would be home for a visit one day. His parents stood a moment in shock, they were both speechless and they told him so. His father told him "come home anytime soon, you are always welcomed. It's been twenty-five years since you've been back and we would love to have you. But a few things have changed, we turned your room into a music room and we gave all your toys to your nephew's years ago, but we kept your teddy bear" they all laughed.

Peterson hugged his mother again and when his father was out of ear shot, Peterson whispered to his mother "mama, I'm coming back home for good, I want to come home and take care of you and daddy"

Peterson's mother hugged him back and laughed "thank you, baby, but me and your daddy are just fine; we take care of each other. How 'bout you coming back and we'll take care of you? We'll find you a good woman and you and your lady can come by every Sunday for dinner"

Before Peterson's mother got on the plane, she said "I'll tell your daddy what you said on the plane, baby and we'll see you real soon"

....

Back at his home Peterson took a look around his house that now seemed way too big for him. He grew tired of living alone and yearned for a relationship and someone to call his own. He still couldn't believe that he told his mother that he would be coming back to Cincinnati to live, but at that moment in the airport, he realized that he had everything a man could want. He had everything but family.

....

It took Peterson six days' drive from Seattle to Cincinnati. Peterson stopped along the way in Salt Lake City, Omaha to visit family, Chicago to take in the sights and then on to Cincinnati.

Back in Cincinnati (or what Peterson referred to as the big Mayberry, surrounded by little Mayberry's), he navigated the streets with a map of Ohio. So much was as he remembered, but so much had changed. The highway now went through the west end and what used to be Sixth Street was no longer and the people were moved out to Madisonville. Making his way from downtown, he passed Sears, Peoples corner, drove through the communities of Avondale, Walnut Hills, Evanston and Ike's Barbecue. He drove around neighborhoods that used to be all white, surprised to see black faces sprinkled throughout. Cincinnati was the same, but so different, he was in total awe. He found that he really missed his hometown. Missed the hills, the architecture and Reds baseball, the Reds were now world champions and looking to repeat. Man how he missed the green spaces, the river and the parks. He would head to his parents' house, but he had to make a stop first. Peterson had to stop for something he had been craving for twenty-five years, a good ole home cooked meal from Newton's.

CHAPTER 14

DEJA VU

Rodney was sitting on the edge of the pool. He was slowly moving the water around with his feet, making figure eights and circles. He looked up to the sky, the sun shone bright. He knew that the water would be freezing cold once he decided to make the plunge. But for now the warm eighty-five-degree breeze felt good tickling his skin and warming his face.

The mid-summer sky was so clear and so blue. The clouds looked like hippos and elephants made of huge cotton balls floating across the sky.

He closed his eyes soaking in the sun. The light breeze had died and he could feel himself starting to sweat.

Rodney didn't move when the sun gave way to shadows, but opened one eye slowly, then the other.

"Have you been waiting long" his mother asked

"No, not too long Rodney replied. "I was just sitting here thinking and getting psyched up"

"What's my little chip monk thinking about and what are you getting psyched up about?"

"I was thinking that today is the day that I am going to swim from one this end of the pool to the other and back non-stop" Rodney said in a casual tone.

"Really Chip, are you sure? You know that the other end of the pool is deep and really far away. You will have to pace yourself in the deep end if you are going to make it"

"I know and I am ready, you can watch me from here, okay. Don't worry, I will be right back"

"I'll walk along the side of the pool while you swim to the other end and back. I will say encouraging words and cheer you on, just like you were in a big swimming event. Would you like that?"

"Yeah, I would really like that" Rodney said smiling for the first time.

"Hey, I just wanted to let you know how proud I am of you and I know you can make it to the other end in no time. Try not to make an old lady run"

Rodney stood, ready to jump in, but his mother put her hand lightly on his chest, covering his heart like people do when they say the pledge of allegiance.

He noticed that she was doing that a lot lately, covering his heart with her hand, so he covers her hand with his.

"Mom I noticed that lately when we are together you always put your hand over my heart, why is that?"

"I just want you to know that mommy will always be right here with you, in your heart"

"Okay, but will I be in your heart too?" Rodney asked curiously.

"Of course baby and every other heartbeat will be just for you, okay?"

66

"Okay mommy and every other beat of my heart will beat for you"

Rodney turned to face his mother; she seemed so much shorter now and so frail. He thought that maybe with last year's growth spurt and the few pounds of muscle made her seem smaller.

"Mom, I am ready to swim to the other side" Rodney said beaming with pride.

"Okay baby. Mommy will be with you the whole time"

Rodney grinned and dove into the pool. He already knew that he could swim the full length of the pool, down and back.

On the days when his father was not too tired or could get out of work a little early, he would meet Rodney at the pool and teach him to swim laps. Neither Rodney nor his father told his mother about this, Rodney wanted this to be a big surprise for his mother.

As Rodney made his way through the water of the deep end, he could hear his mother's words of encouragement. She was cheering so loud that he could hear her clearly when he swam underwater.

His strokes were steady and strong. He was breathing in between strokes and pacing himself, just like his father told him. When he reached the deep end and made his turn back for the shallow end, he could see the sun and the silhouette that it cast on his mother as she walked the sideline.

He smiled inside knowing that this was making his mother so proud. So proud that she must be running the sidelines with the pace that he was keeping.

Rodney makes it to the shallow end of the pool and looks up to see the sun again and the silhouette of his mother, he can't see her face, but he knows that she is probably laughing and crying at the same time. Besides holding her hand to his heart, he noticed that lately she is crying a lot.

Rodney tells his mother "I am going for another lap, mommy, wait for me!"

He turns and starts to swim toward the deep end again. This time the water seems to be a little choppy and the wind has picked up. He puts his head above water, but can no longer see the other end. He goes under water, because at five foot nine and the deep end being six foot, he can just bob to the side. As he goes under his feet are not touching bottom. He is thinking, there is no way he made it to the twelve foot, he wasn't swimming that fast. He makes his way back to the surface and when he looks around he doesn't see his mother or the edge of the pool, it is like he is in the ocean. He calls out, but no answer. He is scared now and doesn't know which way to go. He swims harder and faster, looking for something to grab onto. He feels pressure on his chest and knows that he must be sucking in a lot of water. He wants to yell out, but can't because the water is rushing into his mouth. He slows his breathing and remembers what his father told him "don't fight the water, just go with it, relax and you will float to the top"

He is now on top of the water on his back floating, just like his father taught him. He still feels pressure in his chest, but it doesn't hurt, it actually feels soothing and very peaceful. It feels like when his mother puts her hand to his chest.

He takes a shallow breath, then a deeper breath and finally a big deep breath. He has finally calmed down and his breathing is right. He feels around and notices that he is touching something solid. He is on dry land, he opens one eye slowly, then the other. As he is looking up, his mother is looking down on him smiling. This time he can see her face, her dimples, her big eyes and the warm crooked smile that she always smiles. Rodney smiles back as his mother touches his chest. He puts his hand on top of hers.

"You are such a strong young man now and I am so proud of you, you will be fine now. I love you and always will" she says in a voice that was just above a whisper.

"I love you too mommy, let's go home now" Rodney whispered back.

"You are home baby. Promise me you'll look after your father for me. Let him know that I am fine and I will always love him. Tell him that it is so sweet that he doesn't sleep on my side of the bed, but let him know that it is alright if he sleeps on my side of the bed too" She smiled and said "I love you baby, good night"

"I love you too mommy and I will take care of Daddy and tell him everything you said" Then Rodney drops off to sleep.

....

Rodney sits straight up and looks around; there is no sun and no water. He is in his own bed, it is drenched with sweat. He looks around and sees the sliver of light coming from under the bathroom door. The light he uses as a night light.

Now he is fully awake, wondering if that was a dream because it felt so real. He puts his hand on his chest and thinks he feels his mother's hand. The room is empty, but he can feel a soft breeze that smells like citrus and other fruits. That was the smell of his mother's perfume.

Rodney slowly gets out of bed and pads across the carpet in his room to the hallway. Once in the hallway he stops to look out of the big window on the staircase landing. It's still dark outside with barley any light from the moon.

He decides to look in on his father, just like he promised his mother. He walks to his father side of the bed and notices for the first time that his father does only sleep on one side of the bed. His mother's side is untouched.

Rodney puts his hand on his father's shoulder, he wants to tell him about his dream ready to wake him, but his father is already awake, looking towards the window. His father says "hey son, guess you couldn't sleep either"

"No Sir, I had another dream about mom. Are you doing alright?"

His father says in a barely audible voice "I'm making it son, how are you doing"

"Fine daddy, I mean, I am doing good. I had the swimming dream again and mom was there watching me."

His father smiles and looks to the other side of the bed. "I know, she watches me too, I feel her"

"Daddy mommy made me promise to look after you, I am to tell you that she is fine and you need to sleep. She says that you can sleep on her side of the bed too, it would make her happy"

"Sounds just like something your mother would tell me" his father chuckled.

Rodney's father reaches out and hugs him. He hugs him so tight that Rodney can barely breathe. Rodney likes the way his father hugs and hugs him back just as tight. They both look at the made up side of the bed that was his mother's side. They look at her picture on the night stand. What a gorgeous woman, the dimples, big eyes and the crooked smile. It is like she is smiling at both of them with the pride that she always had for her men.

A tear streams down his father's face. Rodney lets a tear or two run himself. His father says softly, "hey remember we promised your mother that there would be no tears, we would only think happy thoughts"

"Yes sir"

"Hey speaking of happy thought, remembers the lady named Cookie that your mother used to talk about all the time. The girl she grew up with and they were always getting into trouble"

"Yes sir, I remember"

"Well son, Cookie is Ms. Norwell, your young lady friend's mother. How's that for coincidence? Cookie would come visit your mother almost every day while you and her girls were at school. Her husband Mr. Norwell always tried to keep those two apart, said your mama was a bad influence on his woman, but they would sneak and visit every chance they got. Your mother once gave Mr. Norwell a black eye after a high school basketball game. Your mother was on the drill team and carried her baton

70

everywhere. One night after a basketball game Jay Norwell said something to your mother and Cookie that set your mother off. She swung that baton hard and hit Jay Norwell right in the eye, knocking him off the bleachers, he tried to catch himself and sprained wrist. He had to sit out two basketball games and sport that shiner for about a week. Your mother was a feisty woman, who didn't take crap from no one, not even me. She kind of reminded me of your little lady friend, Cola? Kim? Is that her name? Your mama had much attitude and used to cuss up a storm too."

Rodney looked at his father with big eyes and amazement, "mom was like Kim?"

"Yes, she was, maybe even worse, we'll talk more later, but right now we'd better get some sleep. Hey son, I'm glad we got to talk and I promise, I will do a lot better and from this point forward. It felt good to see Cookie and talk with you about your mother, have a good night son, I love you" his father smiled.

"Thanks, dad, love you too" Rodney patted his father on the shoulder and left the room feeling better. Rodney stopped to look out of the big window on the landing of the stairs. The clouds had given way to the bright half-moon and the house was now lit up by the moon.

As Rodney tuned to go into his room, he could hear the soft snoring coming from his father's room down the hall. He tried to remember the last time he heard his father fall into a deep enough sleep that would bring on snoring. Tonight it was very soothing and comforting to know that his father finally found peace with his mother's passing. Tonight was the first time his father spoke of his mother since her passing two years ago.

Rodney smiled to himself, knowing that everything was going to be just fine. Tomorrow, he would talk to "Cookie" and see what she and his mother were like as kids.

He got down on his knees on the side of the bed and said a little prayer for his mother, father, Ms. Cookie, Ty, Regina and Kim. He then slid back under the covers and fell fast asleep.

CHAPTER 15

BRAINSTORM

Rodney was up before the alarm went off, he lay in bed thinking of the talk he had with his father the night before. It was always nice to dream about his mother, but this was the first time that he mentioned his dream and then actually talked with his father about his mother.

After he left his father's room Rodney had another pleasant dream about his mother. The last dream was about him helping his mother in the kitchen cooking and ended shortly before the alarm went off. He turned the alarm off and he decided to jump out of bed and get the day started.

Rodney was up, cooked breakfast for himself and left his father a plate of cheese eggs on the stove with a few slices of bacon and toast. He showered and even made his bed this morning. This was unusual because Rodney was a hard sleeper and it usually took six snooze buttons and his father's urging to get up and get ready for school,

Rodney was about to grab his key and head out the door when his father came into the kitchen. Rodney greeted his father "Hey pops, I left you some food on the stove and started the coffee, I wasn't sure how much coffee to use, so I put in three scoops"

His father poured a cup of coffee and it was actually pretty good and he let Rodney know and thanked him. "Where are you off to so early, son?"

"I promised Kim that I would see her before school" Rodney replied.

"Alright, don't you go being a burden to Ms. Cookie" his father warned.

"I promise, I won't" Rodney said as he made his way out the door, "Love you, pops" and he was gone.

....

Rodney and Regina reached the Norwell house about the same time. He and Regina met at the curb and Rodney reached out and patted her afro while Regina went in for the hug that Rodney knew was coming, but hadn't figured out to avoid yet.

At the end of the hug, Regina playfully punched Rodney in the kidney and said "What's happening Rodney, are you going to walk us to school every day?"

"I guess so" Rodney said nonchalantly.

Ty was at the door when Rodney and Regina walked up, they all said their hellos and Ty invited them in. The house smelled of bacon and eggs, Ty told Rodney to have a seat and she would get Kim as Regina gave her a hug.

Rodney asked, "Ty is your mother in the kitchen, I would like to talk to her for a second?"

"Yeah, she's back there, go on back" Ty answered while looking at Regina, like what's up with this. Ty yelled up the stairs for Kim as Rodney made his way to the kitchen.

"Good morning Ms. Cookie, how are you doing today?" Rodney asked with a big smile on his face.

Tanya turned from looking out the back door, looked at Rodney while she gave Regina a hug and asked Rodney "what did you call me?"

"Ms. Cookie, my pops said that was the nickname that my mother gave you when you were a kid" Rodney smiled wider

"Oh my goodness, I don't believe anyone but your mother has called me that since junior high school, young man you just made me feels like a kid again" Mama laughed and gave Rodney a big hug.

"When I was younger my mother would always tell me these stories about how Cookie did this and Cookie and her did that. She said you two were always in trouble"

Just then Kim walked in and asked "who's Cookie and why was she always in trouble? What's happening Rodney? hey Regina" Kim gave Regina her morning hug.

"Apparently Mama is Cookie and her and Rodney's mother were trouble makers" Regina said in an accusing tone.

Mama leaned against the sink and put her hands on her hips and playfully scolded Rodney "your mother was the only person to call me that name and live to tell about it. Your mother and I were good kids and hardly ever got into trouble" mama said that while trying to keep a straight face.

"So mama, why did she call you Cookie? Ty asked with a mouth full of food.

"Ms. N, that's a cute nickname, I wish I had a nickname" Regina added

"You do have a nickname, we call you knot head all the time" Rodney laughed and tugged at Regina's afro.

"Anyway" Regina said dismissing Rodney "tells us some stories about you being a kid, Ms. N, I guess I never thought of you as ever being young, I mean a girl, well a teenager, you know what I mean. Tell us how you got the nickname Cookie"

Mama laughed and said "I'll tell you, then it is off to school you all go. When me and Rodney's mama were real young, younger than you all, your mama decided that we needed nicknames. There were a couple of sisters that everyone called peaches and pumpkin and a set of twins that the kids nicknamed Minnie and Mickey, oh and these two girls called themselves Pixie and Dixie like the mice on cartoons. Rodney's mother came up with the idea that we should have nicknames. She would call me Cookie and I was to call her sweets. For a short time a few of the girls we knew called us cookie and sweets. But, thank goodness those nicknames didn't stick. The only people to every call me Cookie were Rodney's mother and father and his grandmother. Mr. Norwell hated that nickname" Mama looked at me and smiled.

"Rodney your mother did have a nickname though, everyone called her Luv. It was short for Lavonia, her God given name.

"How did you meet my mother?" Rodney asked.

Mama looked at the clock and then at Rodney "I met you mama when we were toddlers, your mama lived on the floor above us when we lived downtown in the projects. Our mothers became good friends when our fathers went off to work. My father was a porter on a train and your grandfather was a truck driver. When our fathers earned enough money they bought houses one block apart, your grandparents back yard butted up to Ty and Kim's Grammy's backyard. Your grandmothers would meet at the back fence and they would pass me and your mother back and forth over the fence so we could play while they talked. As we got older, your mama used to climb the fence and show up at our back door every morning at 7:30, school or not" Mama smiled as she recalled the memories.

"Like Regina, mama" Ty asked

"Just like Regina" mama said as she put her around Regina's shoulder and kissed her forehead.

"Ms. Cookie, can you tell me more about my mama?" Rodney beamed

"Yes honey anytime, but now you all have to go to school, you're going to barely make it on time" mama said as she took Rodney's face in her hands like she always did to me and Ty. She looked him in his eyes and mumbled, "My goodness if you don't look just like your mama. Luv is this you, are you in there? You sent this boy here calling me Cookie, this is your doing, you just gonna make that darn nickname stick ain't you? If you're in there, Luv, come out now" then mama knocked on Rodney's head like she was knocking on a door.

"I will tell you anything you want baby, anytime, but right now you all need to get out of here" Mama was saying as she gave Rodney a hug and walked us all to the door.

At the door Mama looked over Ty, Regina and Rodney and told them how nice they looked in their catholic school attire. Then she looked over to me and my brother Michael who just walked up and shook her head.

Michael and I said in unison "what?" Michael was wearing a green army field jacket with a dirty hooded sweat jacket underneath, the hood hanging over the collar, a pair of huge bell bottoms, three-inch platform shoes and a flipped up hat like JJ from the show Good times wore. I was wearing my red converse high tops with yellow and white shoe laces in each shoe, a jean skirt, a red tee shirt with a waist length jean jacket with my name Kim in marker across the back. I had my hair in afro puffs that were tied with red and yellow ribbons. I was already popping my first piece of bubble yum.

Mama shook her head and said "maybe the two of you need to go to catholic school, just so that you can dress nicer everyday"

We all hugged mama one at a time and headed out the door and she told us all to have a good day and to be good in school.

I heard Michael say under his breath "if I make it to school"

CHAPTER 16

CHILLIN

I was sitting on the porch swing watching the kids in the neighborhood play on our front lawn.

Rodney, his cousin Johnny and a few of the boys who lived on my block were playing a game they called smear the queer. One boy would throw the football high in the air, and then the boys would wrestle for the ball. The boy who wound up with the ball would run until the other boys caught and tackled him. Then the boy who was tackled would throw the ball high in the air to start the game all over again. They seemed be having fun. Ty, Regina and a couple of girls from her school were jumping double Dutch and singing songs. They seemed to be having just as much fun as the boys. Me, I was bored to tears.

Mama came to the door with refreshments for everyone. She had a pitcher of Kool-Aid and a variety of cookies. Mama looked at me sitting on the swing and asked "are you in another one of your melancholy moods, baby? Why don't you hand out refreshments to everyone maybe that will change your mood" I did as mama asked, but I didn't feel any better.

After Rodney's cousin Johnny finished his drink and cookies, I told that I spit in his drink and dropped his cookies in the dirt. He looked at me and held out his cup "waitress, give me more Kool-Aid, hold the spit and try not to drop my cookies in the dirt this time" What a jerk.

After snacks everyone sat on the porch chilling. The boys talked sports, the girls talked clothes and in between they all talked music. I had enough of this and I needed to get off this porch. I went to the kitchen and asked mama if I could go to the store and buy some gum. Mama told me I could go to the store and gave me a list of things to get at the super market. Before I reached the door, she told me to take someone with me. I walked out on the porch and said "Rodney, mama said you have to come with me to the store to get some stuff"

The boys teased Rodney about going to the store with me, but it didn't faze him. The girls thought it was nice that Rodney didn't mind. Rodney's cousin Johnny was leaning on the rail making his usual snide remarks. I reached down and picked up the football and threw it as hard as I could and the ball hit him square on the back. He turned around really fast and told Rodney "man, you'd better get your girl"

I looked at Johnny and asked "or what? What are you gonna do? Little punk" I turned on my heels and headed back towards the porch. I wasn't going anywhere because Rodney had me by the belt and was pulling me towards the street. I yelled at Johnny "you better not be on my porch when I get back or I'm kicking your ass"

Rodney was still tugging me by the belt and laughing. I spun around quickly and we bumped heads. I reached up and rubbed his head telling him that I was sorry and he rubbed my head and asked if I was alright. Then he had the nerve to say "why are you always picking with Johnny? Do you like him?" I told Rodney "hell no, I don't like your cousin, he gets on my last nerve. What's your problem, you act like you're jealous and shit" as soon as those words came out, I wished I could take them back. I looked down at the ground and said "I just don't like the way your cousin treats you, Rodney"

We walked to the store in silence. I could tell he wasn't happy with me and I deserved it.

In the store we looked at the small list mama gave us and tore it in half. Rodney walked toward the produce section and I headed for the dairy. I turned and said "meet you at the cereal" but Rodney walked away and didn't look back.

I grabbed a box of butter and was headed for the milk when I saw a very tall man, who was dark skin with very white teeth. He had his basket in one hand and his hat in the other, his hair was short with a part on the left side and he was dressed in a suit like he was going to church. He smiled at me and said "hello young lady, how are you today" I returned his smile and said "I'm fine and how are you, older man?" I usually don't speak to strangers, but this man wasn't a stranger, he was someone that I thought I knew, but couldn't place him, but I knew it would come to me.

His laugh was deep and his smile was big, he said "I am doing very well thank you"

I replied "that's good and since you are standing there, could you make yourself useful and hand me the jug of milk up there with the blue cap? My mama likes the two percent milk, but I like the regular milk"

He got the milk from the upper shelf with no effort. I reached up and took the jug from his hands. He looked at my puzzled, so I said "I knew I would find you, I told them I would see you again. My name is Kim and that guy coming over is my friend Rodney" I pointed to Rodney as he made his way up the aisle. I was so nervous and happy that I was giggling and I never giggle. Rodney looked at me and then looked at the man and he stood between the two of us looking like he was ready to fight. Rodney asked me if I was alright. I put my hand on his shoulder, he was jealous and in defense mode. I said to Rodney "I'm fine. This is the man I told you about; uh what's your name mister?"

"Mitchell", the man said, "I'm Peterson Mitchell, Do I know you?" The man looked confused and Rodney was getting pissed.

"Well, kind of, not really, well not yet" I was stumbling over my words and speaking a mile a minute. I took a deep breath and said "you are the man from the diner, you bought us lunch. You were staring at my mother the whole time that you were eating. It was a few weeks ago and you paid for our lunch. My mama cried because you were so nice to us. Mama said it was only a random act of kindness, but I told her it was destiny and that the two of you were meant to be together because "the gift" told me you were going to meet again. Mr. Pete, you have to meet my mother, she is nice and beautiful, well you know, you've seen her and she'll want to thank you for buying our lunch. You can come by the house and meet mama; we only live a few blocks away. It is the big yellow house on the corner, you can't miss it, me and Rodney will be sitting out front by the blue mail box.

Rodney and Mr. Peterson looked at me like I was growing horns. "What's the problem?" I asked.

"Well, Kim is it? I really don't know what to say. I remember the diner and I remember buying you all lunch, but if memory serves me right, your mother didn't seem too receptive to me approaching you all"

"Look Mr. Pete" I started, not knowing where I was going with this. "My mama cried when you bought our lunch, the least you can do is let her thank you in person. My mama and daddy divorced five years ago and my mama hasn't spoken to a man since. I know she liked you, because she smiled for days after we saw you in the diner and mama ain't smiled in years. I overheard mama telling my Grammy that you were a very handsome man with a nice smile. I ain't lying"

Mr. Peterson looked at Rodney for help. Rodney put his hands up and shook his head, letting Mr. Peterson know that he was on his own.

I was still pleading my case for mama when we reached the checkout. I was telling him how mama played sports in college and that she has a degree in helping athletes with their muscles. I was just about to tell him about mama roller skating and dancing when Rodney spoke. "Look brother, Kim's not going to stop talking until she gets her way. If I was you, I would at least go meet Ms. Tanya. Ms. Tanya is really a nice lady and I did hear her talk about the guy who bought them lunch a couple of times" Rodney smiled at me and winked.

Mr. Peterson looked at Rodney, then looked at me as he handed the cashier two ten dollar bills for his groceries. He told the cashier that he would pay for everything and to put our purchase in a separate bag. When I heard that he was paying I laid two more blow pops and a pack of hubba bubba gum on the conveyor. I was liking this man more and more by the minute.

Chapter 17

LOVE WONT LET ME WAIT

We were now standing in the parking lot next to Mr. Peterson Mitchell's nice, new fancy sports car. I was telling him that I had a change of plans. He was to drive the few blocks and park by the mail box. Rodney and I would meet him there. Then I would go in the house and bring mama out to meet him. We all agreed this would be the best way to introduce them. I gave him directions one more time, and then pointed him in the direction of our house. I told him that we would be there in a few minutes. He looked to the heavens through his open tee top in the roof of his car and said "Lord, you really do work in mysterious ways" He started the car engine and slowly backed out his spot. He looked over at Rodney and me and gave us thumbs and the peace sign. I gave him thumbs up back, then a Miss America wave and the cutest, most innocent smile that I could muster. He had a look on his face that said he couldn't believe that he was being fixed up with a woman he has never met, by a determined little kid who hemmed him up in the grocer's freezer.

I looked at Rodney and smiled. Rodney looked at me, smiled and shook his head. We both laughed then Rodney said "you know your mama is going to be pissed, she's going to kill you"

"I know, but …." I said in a serious tone and looked the ground and kicked a loose rock. "Rodney, this had to be fate or my gift working its magic. Check this out. At approximately three PM, I get a craving for a blow pop. While in the kitchen at that same exact time, mama runs out of milk and eggs for the cornbread. Two minutes later, I happen to walk in the kitchen to bum a nickel from mama. Before I get in the kitchen good mama says "I was just coming out to get you and send you to the store" I tell her that I was just coming to see if I could get a nickel and go to the store for a blow pop. Mama then says, she will buy me a blow pop if I go to Kroger. I tell mama that I was just going to go to the candy store on the next corner, but instead mama insist that I go to Kroger. I then tell mama that I will go to Kroger, if she buys me and you a blow pop, a pickle and a Tiger Red cream soda.

"Wait, when you came out on the porch, you told me your mama said that I had to go to the store with you" Rodney reminded me.

"Rodney, that doesn't matter, but anyway…." I said dismissing Rodney with a wave of my hand. So where was I, oh yeah, destiny and how all this was meant to be. So, when I go to reach for the eggs, who just happens to be in the dairy case buying eggs, Mr. Peterson, the man who bought us lunch at the diner. See Rodney, the stars made us have an argument. That argument made us split the list and you went to the left, and destiny sent me to the right. Thus Putting me in that dairy case at the exact moment in time that Mr. Peterson Mitchell, the man who bought us lunch just happened to be there.

Coincidence Rodney, I think not. This is cupid working her magic. Predetermined destination, a meeting for love.

Rodney rubbed his chin and thought for moment before speaking. "OK, Kim, if this is a predetermined destination for a meeting of love, why didn't Cupid send your mother to the store to meet this guy?"

I stopped walking, folded my arms and rolled my eyes "See Rodney, I knew it, you don't understand how love works. It's just not that simple" Rodney stopped and looked at me confused. I stared back at him and said in mocking voice that sounded like Goofy "why didn't cupid just send your mama to the store?" What an idiot.

As we walked toward the house, Rodney was asking me how I was going get mama out of the house for this surprise meeting. How would I calm her down once she figured out she was tricked and how would I explain that not only did we talk to a stranger, but we took money and candy from him?

We rounded the last corner and parked at the mail box near our house was the shiny new car with Mr. Peterson Mitchell sitting inside. He was listening to Kool and the Gangs Jungle Boogie and looking a little nervous. I asked "are you nervous" and he responded, "No I'm cool"

Good at least that made one of us. When I left Rodney's side and headed toward the house, I was thinking that this could be the biggest mistake of my life.

....

Just my luck, as I started up the walk toward the house mama had stepped out on the porch and sent Ty and Regina in to get cleaned up. I guess the other kids went home for supper. She was wiping her hands on her apron and looking around. Mama asked me "where are my groceries and who is that Rodney is talking to?"

Darn, I forgot to get the bag from Rodney. Well here it goes. "Mama, don't be upset, but that's the man from the diner who bought us lunch that day. He was buying eggs at the same time that I was and we recognized each other and well, you said that you would like to thank him one day"

Mama took my hand in hers and we started walking toward the street. Mama's hand was so soft and a little wet and she wasn't tugging me, we were just walking. I looked up at mama and said "his name is Mr. Peterson Mitchell. And he is really nice" Mama looked down at me, smiled and said "Mr. Mitchell, huh"

By the time we reached the car, Mr. Mitchell was out and standing on the sidewalk a few feet away from the mailbox and Rodney was standing next to him. It was funny because they both looked very nervous.

Mr. Mitchell reached out his hand and said "hello, my name is Peterson Mitchell" Mama said "hello, my name is Tanya Mitchell" they shook hands and stood for a moment and smiled at each other.

Mama started by saying how thankful she was for his kindness and thoughtfulness for buying our meal that day. Mr. Mitchell said it was his pleasure. He explained that it was nice to see a family having a nice meal together. He told mama that he wasn't trying to be forward or pry, but he did ask the waitress about her and the waitress told him that our family came in often and we were one of her best customers. The waitress also mentioned that in the last four years that she worked there, it was usually just mama and the kids and she heard that mama was divorced. Mr. Mitchell told mama that he was sorry about the divorce as his smile got a little wider.

They were talking a mile a minute, sometimes talking over each other. During the conversation each had said "oh no, you go first or I'm sorry, please continue" The conversation was going nicely and it was as though they forgot me and Rodney were there, until mama stepped to the side and bumped into me. She told me and Rodney to go in the house and wash up because the food was already done and we would be eating soon.

As we made our way to the house Rodney said "I can't believe it, your mama was all grins and giggles, she wasn't mad at all, actually she seemed really happy"

"I know" I said surprised. "Did you hear the way they were talking a mile a minute. Mama was like a little girl. He is a really nice man" When Rodney and I reached the porch, we stood and looked out to the street, and mama and Mr. Mitchell were both leaning on the car in full conversation. I guess I should have told Rodney "I told you so" and "I was right and he was wrong", but at this moment, it didn't matter, it was nice to see mama smile and talk to a man other than my father.

CHAPTER 18

PAYBACK IS A DOG

It was early Sunday morning and Tanya was just waking up from a good night sleep. She was remembering the dream she had shortly before she awoke. She was slow dancing with Marvin Gaye on soul train and they were on stage singing "Ain't nothing like the real thing" She was wearing hip huggers that accentuated her tight rear end, a halter top that showed just enough cleavage to keep Marvin's eyes going up and down the length of her body and just enough skin in the tummy area that kept Marvin's hands caressing her mid-section. Damn he was so fine and so sexy; she would be his any day.

Tanya looked at the clock; it was five in the morning. She was still a little tired, but figured it was time to get a move on, there were chores to be done and kids to rise. Marvin would have to wait until tonight to "get it on" with her. Tanya made her early morning rounds moving slowly past the girl's room. She looked in on them briefly, they were fast asleep, both in Ty's bed. Tanya figured the storm last night must have scared Kim and she went to sleep with her sister. Tanya knew that Kim was scared to death of thunder and lightning, but would never admit it, she would turn it around and say that Ty was scared, so she slept in the bed with her. The two girls looked so peaceful, like little angels. In a couple of hours they would be at each other's throats and causing five kinds of hell. Tanya took in the scene a little longer and put her hands in front of her face like she had a camera and was snapping a picture.

Next Tanya made her way to her son Michael's room, lately they had been at odds with each other and Tanya felt that a lot of it was her fault. He was no longer mama's little boy. He was now in high school and fast becoming his own man. Tanya felt that she did a good job raising him as a young boy, but she was lost on how to raise a young man? This is where his father is supposed to step in and take over. Teach the young man about hygiene. Show him how to tie a tie, how to shave and how to dress. Show him how to act and present himself properly in the presence of his elders. How can you be cool in the company of young women? Let the boy know that life will not be fair or easy for a man of color. Tell his son about finances and the importance of saving. Open the door to success for him, he may not walk through it, but at least he would be shown the path. Man up and do the job of a father.

Tanya was at Michael's room door, the door was shut as usual. She reached down and touched the knob wondering if she should knock or just walk in. She decided to just look in on him for a second and hopefully not disturb him. She turned the knob and cracked the door just a bit. She was hoping to catch a glimpse of his angelic face that resembled his two sisters. She saw a face alright, but it wasn't a boy's face, it was a girl's face with long braids, the little slut from down the street. That girl had to be at least eighteen and just a junior in high school. This was the girl she had warned him about, forbid him to see and stressed to him over and over that she was nothing but trouble. Tanya slowly closed to door and took a deep breath, counted to ten and tried to remain calm, but none of this was working for her. She was so mad, she couldn't see straight and she didn't want to overreact. Over react, this boy had brought a stranger into her home, with her daughters in the next room! After what seemed like an eternity in the hallway, Tanya said to herself in a low deep voice, not in my house, not here in my damn house. Tanya didn't remember walking through the door or jumping on the bed, but here she was on top of the bed, straddling her son and the tramp from down the street. It took all she had not to yell.

Tanya leaned down putting her head as close as she could stand to the two of their faces; they reeked of cheap wine, cigarettes and marijuana. She slowly said "What the hell do you two think you are doing in my damn house. Wake the hell up and look at me. Don't neither of you speak and you better not wake my babies. I should kill you both where you lay.

Michael woke up with a start. He started to say "mama, what the fuck..." but the punch to the mouth made him close his eyes and turn his head. The tramp from down the street looked up at Tanya and let out a little shriek just as Tanya's hand closed around her throat. Tonya spoke very slowly and in a threatening tone "I am only going to say this once more, if you wake my girls I will kill you both" She looked at her son with crazed eyes. Dammit, he looked just as his father did the day she came home early and caught him screwing another woman on their bathroom floor.

Michaels face was contorted with a look of shock and terror. He was looking at a woman he did not recognize. This was not his mother; this deranged lady who punched him and cursed was someone he did not know. He felt he must be dreaming, but the pain and blood from his split lip seemed so real.

Tanya continued in a low gruff voice that she didn't recognize "what the hell is wrong with you disrespecting me and my house. You are freaking ingrate. You have two little sisters who look up to you, they don't need to see this, and I should kill you" Then Tanya looked to the frightened girl. The caked on makeup she wore the night before was smeared on the pillow case, Tanya could see that she wasn't near as old as she assumed when she saw her on the street. The girl, up close appeared to be about fifteen, not much older than her own daughters.

Tanya wanted to feel bad for the girl, but couldn't. She slowly releases the grip on the girl's neck and asked, "How old are you?"

The girl squeaked "sixteen, same age as Michael"

Tanya shuddered and closed her eyes; she was so mad and disgusted that she wanted to scream. Tanya continued in her low threatening voice "why are you doing this to yourself? you dress and act like a whore, you look so much older than sixteen with all this clown makeup on your face. You are doing drugs, sleeping around doing God knows what, with God knows who. What in God's name is wrong with you?"

Tanya then turned on her oldest child and asked "What? What have I done so wrong that you feel that you have to do drugs and go against everything good that I have ever taught you?" She raised her hand to hit him again, but he showed a look of defiance. He didn't cry, but his eyes gave away his fear. Tanya did not soften; she would not tolerate his disrespect, not now, not ever. For a few long minutes she stared him down. Let him know with her stare that enough was enough.

Tanya ran her hands over her lopsided afro and said"so it's like this, you think you're the man of this house. I would love for you to have a father figure around, but for now mister, you just have me. I am so tired of the truancy from school, the drinking, the drugs and your attitude that I just want to cry. But just like your father, tears and emotions mean nothing to you. There was a long pause and Tanya took a cleansing breath and said calmly "I want you out of my house, call your father, call your grandmother, I don't care who you call, you have to go"

Tanya slowly slid off the bed and headed toward the door, slowly turning her back on the kids. She paused with her hand on the knob when Michael whispered "Mama, wait"

Michael spoke in a hushed tone "I don't want to go, but you are right, I need to get out. I feel like I am becoming my father and I hate it. I don't want to be like that bastard, I hate everything about him. I'm so sorry mama, I really am. Mama, I don't want to leave you and my sisters, you're all I got. I know I've been acting out but I am just so mad at the world and I don't know why, I'm sorry I hurt you this way, I really am, and I screwed up"

Tanya turned and looked at her only son; she knew she couldn't put her own flesh and blood out on the street. She was thinking to herself, he did not ask to be born, she gave him life, this is not his fault. She and her asshole ex created this child, the two of them as teenagers, not much older than him and the girl in the bed. The two of them (she and her ex) didn't know the consequences of unprotected sex at an early age, but she talked with Michael about sex until she was blue in the face, he knew better.

Tanya finally spoke after a long silence and looked softly at son "I have been thinking about what to do with you for a while. I decided to send you to live with your uncle Lem. I'll call him today and you will be leaving as soon as I can get him up here to get you. Michael, get this young lady out of my house and don't ever bring her back here again. Young lady, my advice to you is to respect and love yourself and I pray God shows you a better way to live your life. You could be a nice looking young lady if you got rid of the makeup and quit acting grown.

Tanya slowly closed the door to her son's room and quietly made her way down the hall, peeking in briefly at the girls who were still hugged up and fast asleep. She thought of going back to the bed where she earlier dreamed happy thoughts, but decided to take a long bath and think.

Engulfed in the tub by water that was way too hot, with too many bubbles and a garden of flowery smells, Tanya starts to cry. She had never thought of spending a waking moment without her son being in the next room or somewhere in the vicinity.

She decided the best thing for her son was to send him hundreds of miles away to live with her take no crap, discipline oriented, drill Sergeant older brother. She figures that if her brother Lem can whip marines into shape, then it should be no problem for him to get her sixteen year old son together and give him a chance at a better life.

Tanya thinks about letting his father know their son will be leaving, but decides that there is no need to let him know since he wasn't here to do his job and make sure their son became a man "screw him" she says in a slight whisper.

Tanya finally gets comfortable and lets the water take her cares away. She says to herself "you are doing the right thing sending Michael to the country with Lem. Lem will take good care of him" She shivers as though she was cold and asks herself, "Michael will be taken care of, I'll make sure the girls are taken care of .... but who will take care of me?"

CHAPTER 19

CLOSE THE DOOR

Grammy was sitting on the end of the sectional closest to the door, knitting and humming a church hymn. I was on her left, sitting between her and my mama. Ty was sitting on the other side of mama, mama always separated us on account if we sat together we would make so much noise that no one would ever get to hear the television. My brother Michael sat at the other end of the sectional just staring far off into space, probably wishing he was anywhere but here.

Good times just went off and Grammy started talking about the new colored shows that were on television now. Yes, my Grammy still like to be called colored. I on the other hand, like being called a Black person. Something about being black made me proud. Anyway Grammy was talking about shows in the 1960's compared to now in the 1970's.

Grammy put her hand in the air like the preacher did when he wanted silence because he was going to make a point. We all looked at her and Grammy said "let me get on my soap box for a moment. Now, in the 1960's it was rare that you would see colored folk on television, but when you did see one of us on television we were on our best behavior. For example Diahann Carroll when she played in that shows Julia. She was the first black woman on television and she was a nurse. She was well spoken, well dressed and always had her hair nicely done. She was a single mother raising her child and doing very well. She was respected by colored and white folk alike"

Grammy continued "I went to the show yesterday and saw Diahann Carroll in her new movie Claudine, let me tell you, now that was a good movie and she was just a s lovely as she always been. It had an all colored cast. At first I didn't like that she was on welfare with six kids, but she played that part and it was a beautiful movie. I cried my ass off at the end.

Now this show we just watched, this Good times with that boy JJ. I don't much like him. This show is going to set colored folks back one hundred years. That boy is strut tin' around like a damn peacock, talking about Dynamite and being ignorant all the time disrespecting his sister. Next he gonna come out eating fried chicken and watermelon while singing mammy. Not only is the boy ugly as sin, but he is ignorant. Forgive me lord, but I don't usually call my colored people ignorant, but that boy is ignorant. And tonight that Wilona chick said Negro on the television during prime time. Negro please? It was like she was airing colored folk's dirty laundry out on the television for the whole white world to see. As colored folk we should never say things like that, it is degrading and disrespectful. Speaking of degrading, that Flip Wilson shows, I cannot stomach that man when he is dressed like that woman Geraldine. My goodness what kind of image is he showing young colored boys? It is sending out the message that is alright to be homo. Our colored men need to be strong. White folk just love to see our men emasculated. Mark my word, next they'll show dykes and lesbians on the TV. You know women with women. These white folk and the media putting nonsense ideas into our young colored folk's heads. This just turns my stomach.

While I'm on the subject, that George Jefferson character on the white bigot Archie Bunker show really pisses me off. That little sawed off Negro, running around calling white folks honky on national television. I mean to say, is that the best he can do, honky? What the hell he means by that? What's a honky? I have some choice names for white folk that would make a slave master cringe and honky ant one. Honky? Really, if I was white and someone colored man called me a honky, I would laugh in his face. If they put me on that show I would put that white man in his place. It would start off something like this, I would say look here mister, let him think I was being all respectful and shit, then the conversation would turn to something like this. Look a here you inbred, cracker eating, pasty face, trailer trash, mother fu ....

Just then mama yelled "Ma, stop, stop it right now, your starting to go a little overboard. Let's be a little more positive in front of the kids. There is nothing wrong with being black and the shows on television are just for entertainment. Except that all in the family show, I find it very bigoted, but then again I know I can just turn the show off if I don't like it"

"Ma, I can see why the kids like to be called black; it gives them a new identity. I think being called colored s like being lumped in with every other person of color who isn't white. I feel that the kids calling themselves black sets them apart from everyone else. When people look at me they know I am black and I am proud of that. In other cultures Negro means black and it is not offensive when they call us that, they are just stating the obvious, we are black, and Negroes.

As for choices I am glad that young black kids can express themselves, maybe not as much as Kim does, but at least they have a chance to be who they are. I like that the kids are growing their hair out naturally, I like the Afros and I think the afro puffs are cute. I like that the black kids have Soul Train. They can watch kids who look like them show off the latest clothes styles dances. White kids have had Bandstand forever and older whites have Lawrence Welk.

96

Look ma, I know these shows aren't Amos and Andy, but for the most part we are going in the right direction. Fat Albert is a good show for children. Sanford and son is entertaining and funny. Get Christy Love is entertaining and shows young black girls that they can be strong and a police woman if they choose to be. No more being a housewife like June Cleaver.

....

After all the discussions and debates, the family finally settled down and the television was turned off for the night. Mama told us kids to get into our pajamas and brush our teeth, then come down and say goodbye to Grammy.

We did as we were told, even Michael put on his pajamas and came down to say goodbye.

"Mama have you been crying?" Ty asked. We all looked from mama to Grammy and they both fell silent and looked away.

Michael spoke for the first time this evening "What's happening here? What's going on?"

Grammy looked at mama and mama stared back at Grammy. Grammy finally said "OK, I should be the one to tell them. Kids, your Grammy has been having a few aches and pains lately down in my woman regions, so I went to the hospital to get it checked out. The doctor tells me that I may have the cancer in me. They don't know for sure, but they want to take a biopsy of a tumor I have and see if it cancerous. I have to go in for test next week. I was just telling your mama that your Grammy is a tough old bird and I ain't gonna let no cancer slow me down. Plus the doctor says that since we caught it early, there is a good chance that I will be just fine. Worse case, if there is cancer; I can have a hysterectomy to remove all the tumors"

"Grammy, what's a hysterectomy?" I asked in a voice that came out a lot stronger than I felt.

"Child that is when they take out my plumbing" We all gave a blank stare and Grammy continued. "You know, my woman parts, my baby making machine" We all shook our head in unison, even mama.

Grammy stood and we each gave her a big hug, then we all hugged her again in a group hug. She had Michael get her coat from the hallway and as she put it on she told us "I don't want any tears in the end. Like that Roberta Flack song, if something were to happen to Grammy, you all have to keep going, make me proud. That especially goes for you Michael, you been acting up and I think it's time grow up and become a man. Do something to make us all proud. If you all want to shed a tear when I'm gone, don't do it on my account because I have lived a full life and my Lord wants to take today, I'm ready. I know once I leave here that I will be in a better place. I may cry for you all because you still have to live with all this war, crime, racism and foolishness. So don't cry for me, my soul will live on and I'll leave this old body behind. But right now, I'm a little scared, but until the test come back, I ain't gonna worry and I don't want you all to worry either. Grammy will be just fine no matter how the test turn out. I love you all and you my family, so we'll all be strong for one another"

We said our goodbyes. Grammy walked out the door and stood on the porch long enough to adjust her scarf and hat. We all stepped out of the house and stood on the porch. It was cold outside as we stood there in our pajamas watching Grammy walk down the stairs to the street. She had walked the four blocks from her house, now she had to walk back home. We watched her until she made it to the next block and turned left and out of sight.

We stood a few minutes longer, no one speaking. We were thinking the same thought, how would we go on without Grammy?

We all shook from the cold and the thought of losing Grammy and headed indoors to the warmth of the house. Mama locked the door and we turned out the downstairs lights and headed up the stairs. When we made it to the top of the stairs, the phone rang twice and stopped. We all stared at the phone and held our breath. The phone rang twice more and stopped. We all started to breathe, but didn't move. This was the signal from Grammy letting us know that she made it home and everything was fine.

Chapter 20

BABY, I'VE BEEN MISSING YOU

The last few days mama has been acting really depressed and her spirits were low.

Mama was sitting at the kitchen table with her head in her hands. She rubbed her face and looked to the ceiling. She asked to no one in particular, Lord, why me?

Rodney happened to walk in the kitchen just as mama was talking to the Lord.

Hey Ms. Cookie, what's the matter?

Hey Rodney, I was just looking to the Lord, asking him why everything bad seems to be happening to me.

What do you mean Ms. Cookie?

I'm divorced, I may be losing my job, I sent my oldest child away to be raised by my brother, my mother may have cancer, my baby girl is hurt bad, I'm messing up with the only man who ever cared about me, Kim, well, you know, she's a mess, your mother, who was the only person that I could ever tell my problems to is gone .... And here I am telling my problems to a fourteen year old boy. Maybe I should start drinking or doing drugs.

Aw, Ms. Cookie, your life aint so bad. Like my daddy says, you have to just sit back, look around you and take in all that you have. For starters you need to assess what you have. Check it out, from what you told us, you don't like your old job; why not get a new job, something you like? My daddy says that if you love what you do, it's doesn't feel like work.

You have a nice comfortable home.

But what about money? How will I support my family?

Daddy says, if you love your job and do it well, the money will come. For instance math is easy for me and I love numbers. When I get a job, I want to be an accountant, like my father. You are good with kids, why don't you become a pediatrician or open a daycare?

I wish life were that simple Rodney, but I need a job.

Ms. Cookie, take classes at the vocational school or go to college in the evening like Regina's mother. It's best to look for a job while you have a job.

You still have your mother, she is just having a biopsy, the cancer could be benign, you have to hope for the best and leave it in God's hands. Grammy is tough; she said that if there is caner in her, it will need to find a new home, because she's too young and pretty to be losing her hair.

As for Ty, Ty is tough, we talked to her and she said that she can't wait to get back to cheer leading. She said with the cast on her arm she is getting attention from all the boys at school. She said if she knew that a broken arm would have gotten her this much attention, she would have broke her arm years ago.

My mama smiled and said to Rodney, my baby said that? See, what am I going to do; now she is boy crazy.

Your ex-husband, Mr. Novelle was an idiot; my daddy said that when my mama punched him out, that he did it for you, because she couldn't stand to see him doing you wrong. He's dumb as a box of rocks. There would be no way I would have let a woman like you go. Look at you, you are beautiful, you are fine as four movie stars, Pam Grier ain't got nothing on you. You have a big heart and

Now Kim is a whole 'nother story, Tell you what, I will take care of Kim and make sure that she is alright, just like my mother used to look out for you.

CHAPTER 21

LET MAMA SLEEP

Since Michael went down south to live with Uncle Lem, I haven't been sleeping much. I've been having strange dreams that I wake up and walk through the house and find Michael either walking in the hall or sitting in the living room. The other night he was sitting on the edge of my bed. Tonight he is at the kitchen table eating cookies and milk.

I pull up a chair at the table and join him. "Michael, what are you doing here? Shouldn't you be down south with Uncle Lem? Are you back home for good?"

Michael just smiles and slides the pack of cookies to me. He dunks and holds the cookie in the milk until it gets soggy, and then he slurps it into his mouth like he's eating oysters. He wipes milk from his lower lip with his index finger and smiles at me like he knows a something that I don't know.

I ask him "Michael are you high?" I'm staring at him. He looks sober and much older than the last time I saw him. He has hair on his face and the stubble makes his teeth look bigger and whiter than I remember. I look at his hands and they seem much bigger and dirtier with calluses on them. He is so much darker then he was when he lived at home. He is now shaking his head side to side telling me no.

"Then what Michael, cat got your tongue? You can't speak? You know mama is going to be so pissed when she finds out that you ran away from uncle Lem's" Michael is now laughing, but there is no sound. He reaches over and puts a warm hand on my cheek. I am smiling on the outside, but inside I want to cry because I miss my brother so much. Michael stands and opens his arms wide and motions for me to come to him. I get up from the table and start toward him, but he is no longer there. I look around and see that I am no longer in the kitchen. I am sitting up in my bed. I shake myself wondering if this is all a dream or is my gift trying to tell me something. I look across at Ty's bed, she isn't there. I remember that she has moved to Michael's room. I stand and slide my feet into my slipper and head towards the kitchen, hoping to see Michael at the table.

I walk quietly through the house hoping not to wake mama or Ty. I make it down the stairs and remember to step over the one step that creeks, third from the bottom. I go to the kitchen and there is no Michael. I take the cookies off the counter pull two out of the pack and eat them. I sit at the table trying to make sense of the dream. I got nothing. So I check to make sure all the doors are locked and make my way towards the steps.

At the top landing I can hear mama talking in her bedroom. I know she better not have no man in her room at this hour of the night. I went to investigate. I crept to her room door and peeked in, hoping not to catch her and Mr. Pete having sex, that would kill me. I shake that thought from my mind. I see mama and she was down on her knees praying. She just passed the part in the prayer where she prayed the lord her soul to take and was now blessing folks. Damn, mama must be blessing everyone that she's known since birth. When I say my blessing I bless Grammy, mama, Michael, Ty and Rodney, in that order. Piss on everyone else, they just gonna have to make it without my blessings. Damn, mama even blessed daddy. She's a better woman than I am.

I listened as Mama continued her prayer she was saying "This may sound crazy Lord, but I want to thank you so much for sending Peter Mitchell to me. You know I only pray to give thanks to you and the heavens above. I usually never ask for anything. You have given me so much Lord and I accept all that you give me graciously. I know I didn't ask for Pete and you know how many times I tried to send him away. But Lord, you know me best and you knew that Peter Mitchell is what I need in my life.

Now I would like to ask you for a favor. Since you sent this wonderful person my way, please deliver me from evil. I know you are protecting me from the devil that we call satin. I need protection from that devil of a man known as my ex-husband. I forgave Jay years ago and tonight I forgive myself. I am moving on with Peter Mitchell. I fault myself for believing that if I were a good person and treated Jay decently that maybe, just maybe, he would be a part of his children's lives. But that never happened; he is actually drifted further away.

Lord, when my ex husband comes around I often think bad thoughts. You know, sexual thoughts and you got me through those times. Lord, you know that I was also thinking unholy thoughts of a homicidal nature. That was on my bad days. Lord, on my good days, I thought about just knee capping or castrating him. Kidding Lord, just kidding. Thank you very much for not letting me act on my impure thoughts.

Thank you again Lord for Peter Mitchell. I believed in you and you came through with a good man this time. I guess going through it Jay Norvelle was a test of my faith. I almost threw in the towel. Just kidding, I am with on your team forever.

Lord, one more request please. Please look after my middle child Kim, she is really a good person who loves with all her heart and speaks with all her mouth. Please give that child a filter on that filthy mouth.

I turned and slowly walked down the hall to my room, I need to say my prayers.

CHAPTER 22

I'M SO INTO YOU

The last few days in this house have been eerily quiet. Grammy said mama is back to her old melancholy self and Uncle Pete has been avoiding being alone with mama. I think it all has something to do with my Daddy coming around to my brother's welcome home party. Daddy was a little drunk when he showed up and he followed mama around like a little lost dog all day. Come to think of it my father has been coming by the house a little more often since mama and Uncle Pete have been seeing each other on a more intimate level. I am not sure what intimate means, but it must have something to do with sex because when I asked Grammy, she told me to mind my business. The only time Grammy tells me to mind my business is when grown up are talking about sex.

Uncle Pete sat at the kitchen table during the party and took in the scene. He watched mama like he always did, giving her a little smile and a wave from time to time. If he was upset, I couldn't tell. He spoke to all the guest when they entered the kitchen for food. He mixed drinks for the drinkers, fixed plates for the older people and passed out cake and ice cream to the kids.

I grabbed Rodney by the collar and whispered in his ear "something ain't right; Mr. Pete has been in the kitchen for a while and hasn't come out since this party started. And look, Mama is moving from person to person, she hasn't sat still for one moment and where ever mama goes, daddy ain't far behind"

Rodney checked out the room and the whole situation. He was stroking his chin and bobbing his head. Rodney has been doing that a lot lately, since a hair or two popped up on his chin. Rodney told me to sit back and relax and he would get to the bottom of this. I said to myself, "that's my man, Rodney Price detective"

During the next half hour Rodney spoke with mama. He sat in the kitchen and talked with Mr. Pete. He followed my father for a bit and they even spoke. Rodney didn't care much for daddy and talking to him was something he has never done. Rodney then made his way to my brother Michael. They shook hands, slapped five and did some shuckin' and jiving. When they were done Rodney made his way to Ty and Regina. The three of them stood together and watched mama work the room. Regina giggled and pointed at daddy. Rodney finished up with Grammy.

When Rodney finished his questioning, he came to me and said "we need to go outside and talk" he grabbed my hand and we made our way to the picnic table in the back yard. Rodney sat on the table and I sat on the bench next to him leaning on his leg. He tugged on my ponytail and I giggled. "So Mr. detective, what did you find out?" I asked as I turned to look up at him.

Rodney leaned over resting his elbows on his thighs; he stroked his chin, smiled at me and said "looks like you have a big problem on your hands. Apparently your father coming around here so much lately is starting to piss Mr. Pete off. Your mama said your pops is coming around to see your brother, trying to have a relationship with his son. Everyone knows that's a lie, Michael hasn't said two words to your old man since he's been back. Even Mr. Pete told your mama he has yet to see your pops talking to your brother. Your mama told him that Michael just hasn't come around yet. Mr. Pete asked your mama if she still had feeling for your pops. Your mama said no and walked away. Your Grammy told Mr. Pete not to give it a second thought, she said your dad is coming around being an asshole because your mama found her a good man and it ain't him. Grammy told Mr. Pete not to make a scene or it would make him seem petty, so Mr. Pete is keeping a distance from your moms and pops. He's still upset with your mama"

"Then I overheard Mrs. Moody down the street ask your mama if she was getting back with your father, your mama said no, but didn't tell her about Mr. Pete"

"Your brother asked your mama, why your father had to show up? Actually he said why is that mother fucker here and pointed at your pops"

Your mama said that he is your father and you are his son. And if it means anything he wanted to see your brother and talk man to man and maybe have a relationship, if your brother could forgive him.

Your brother told your mother that that ship has long sailed, the only man in his life is Uncle Lem. Lem was there when he was in the streets and needed a father, Lem stepped up, not your pops and now he needs to get the fuck out of his life. He said this loud enough for your father to hear him.

Your brother told your mama that he noticed the way her and your pops were acting, like it was a party for them getting back together. He told your mama that Mr. Pete was a good dude and she better watch it or she'll lose him dealing with that bastard. Then he hugged your mama and told her she needed to forget about your pops and go in the kitchen and see about Mr. Pete.

Now I was fuming."I'M GONNA KILL HIM" I shouted at Rodney. "I'll make him disappear. If he messes up mama and Mr. Pete, I'll kill him. Mama is so happy now and …..." I was so mad I couldn't finish my sentence.

Rodney then put his hand on my shoulder and said softly "Kim, I know you probably want to go in there, make a scene and kill your pops in front of everyone. You would probably chop him into little pieces and give away body parts to the guest. As fun as that would be, I can't let you do that. I would kind of miss hanging out with you while you were in prison. I knew you would be upset, so I asked your Grammy to come and talk to you" and on cue Rodney started to get up as Grammy made her way out the back door and toward the picnic table.

As usual, Rodney was right, I would have stabbed my father fifty-five times, chopped his head off and burned what was left of him right there on the living room floor. He also knew that Grammy was the only one who could stop me from killing him. As Rodney made it to the back door, he turned and did the hand motion for calm down and threw me a peace sign. That made me smile and feel a little better.

Grammy sat right down next to me and said "baby, I don't know if your daddy has roots on your mama or your mama caught a case of the stupid's. Her behavior is inexcusable, but sometimes as women, we listen to stupid shit that men tell us and start falling for the bullshit that they are selling. Your daddy has more than likely been around here the last few days telling your mama that you all need to be a family. And now that your brother is back it would be nice if you all could sit down and talk things out, work as a family unit and learn to love each other. He is telling your mother that he screwed up in the past and if she only gave him another chance, she could see how much he has changed, it's all bullshit. Sounds to me like the other family is ready to pitch his ass to the curb"

"Grammy" I asked, "what makes you think my father said all of that?"

"Because I heard them talking the other day when I was listening through the vent in the basement under the kitchen and when I was eaves dropping on their phone calls. Girl, your Grammy may be old, but I know how to snoop, been doing it for damn near sixty years. I know my daughter and I know when she's about to do something stupid and right now your mama is on the verge of doing something way beyond stupid"

"See child, this is when your Grammy steps in, your mama calls it interfering, but Grammy calls it helping your mama out of harm's way. I'll try to talk sense into her; she'll tell me I'm wrong. I'll slap her around a bit, grab her ear, and maybe pinch her titty to make sure that I have her undivided attention. Oh, she'll be mad at me for a while, but she'll get over it and as always she will thank me later"

"Grammy" I said as I gave her a big hug "you crazy"

"Not as crazy as you think. Child, I see you and that Price boy running around here inseparable, almost like you all livin' in the same skin. Y'all ain't having sex, smokin' refers or shootin' that smack are you? Look at him; he's been watching you from the kitchen table ever since we sat down. He a good boy, you may want to keep him around, he's gonna be something" She kissed me on the cheek, told me to let my mama work out this foolishness with my daddy and she walked into the kitchen and popped Rodney upside the back of the head.

....

Meanwhile the party was breaking up and my father was getting drunker. He asked my mama "remember when we were on the road, I think I was playing in San Antonio, we went to the Alamo and we rode those gondolas on the river walk. That was a great time. Remember us singing with the mariachis, eating tacos and drinking tequila. You almost fell in the river. I don't think I laughed so hard in all my life. We had some really good times didn't we? What happened to us baby, what happened, huh?" The room fell quiet and mamas face started to warm …. Wait, what the hell, was she blushing? Was she thinking about getting back together with this scum?

Grammy was quick to clear the room. She yelled "Listen up everybody, you got to go, If you didn't get a plate, it's too late. Start moving toward the door, you ain't welcome here no more. You ain't got to go home, but you have to get the hell outta here" Within minutes everyone was out the door and Grammy had daddy by the arm wrestling him into someones car and calling him everything but a child of God.

Satisfied with how quickly she cleared the house Grammy said her goodbyes to me, Ty and my brother Michael. She went in the kitchen gave Uncle Pete a big hug, said a few words and walked out the front door without a word to mama.

Mama gave us kids a hug and sent us upstairs, it was only a little after nine, so I asked mama if it was alright for me and Rodney went to play in the basement and she absently said, "yeah, but only for a little while" She looked at Uncle Pete sitting at the kitchen table and headed his way. Mama pulled out a chair and sat at the table next to him; poured herself a glass of the wine he was drinking and said "we need to talk"

. . . .

Rodney and I went to the basement and pulled a wooden box up to the vent that Grammy told me about and started to listen in on mama and Uncle Pete's conversation.

Mama started to speak "Pete, honey, I know what you are thinking and no, I do not want to be with him, he is just the father of my children and I do not want to exclude him from their life. We were married once and we do have a past …."

Pete interrupted "do you love him, if he asked you to go back to him, would you ?"

Mama shot back "No, Pete, it's not like that. I don't want him, I really don't and I know he has another family and other kids with other women, so I don't need the lecture. But honestly, he was the first man I ever loved. And yes, for some strange reason, I do sometimes have feelings for him. I guess I never had a chance to get over him, you know closure.

I thought my life would be a lonely one, raising children and going to work. Then you showed up all handsome and perfect and everything I ever wanted in a man. Now I wonder sometimes if I am ready for a relationship......."

Pete was silent for a long minute, and then he sarcastically says "Oh, I see I am just too perfect, I treat you too well and I love you too much. Now I've become a distraction. It's just something to do in between working your job and raising the kids. I guess it was never really in the plans for me to be your man, because you already have one. I guess being part of this family was out too, because they already have a father"

"Let me get this straight" Pete continued "ex-hubby asshole wins your heart, you do all the right things in a relationship that a wife is supposed to do. You go along loving him thinking it will be until death do you part. You take care of his house and the children that you had together. Then asshole decides that being a responsible adult, doing the right thing and sticking to his vows is no longer what he wants to do, not part of his plan. So he bails on you and the kids. Drops divorce papers on you and runs across town to take up with a woman that he already had kids with while you were married and he and the new wifey live happily ever after or until there is trouble in paradise and he just decides to come back and pick up with you, right where he left off ? Am I close?"

"Pete stop" mama says "You don't understand, it's complicated and I won't ask you to understand. But he is the father of my children.

"Really, you believe that you are the only woman in the world that this has happened to, huh?" We hear Pete walk across the floor. "Please, this is my life story. My Grandmother was dogged by my Grandfather as far back as I can remember. He and his mistress were so blatant with their affair that he moved the woman and her kids four blocks away from my Grandmother house. My father went to school every day knowing that the little girl in his homeroom was his half sister.

My Grandmother would tell people in the neighborhood that he may be with the Jezebel for one night, but he will be with her forever. He knows where his home is and he makes sure the rent is paid and the children have food here at 2040 Ralston Place"

There was quiet for a minute, then Pete said in a low voice "my father, may he rot in hell, would not only cheat on my mother, but would bring me and my sister to the other woman's house to babysit us while he went to the track, the bar or another woman's house. Eventually he left my mother for a woman with a lot more money, started a new family and lived in a nice big house on the other side of town"

I heard a sniffle and couldn't tell if it was my mother or Uncle Pete crying. Pete spoke a little louder this time and said" When I was younger I actually hated my mother for ever loving my father and remaining in a one sided love affair. I thought it was asinine"

We heard Pete stand; he asked my mother if she would like more ice in her drink. My mother said yes and we heard him slowly walk to the refrigerator and get ice. He sat and started talking again "I met my first love at nineteen, we didn't get married, nor did we have children. I treated her very well and tried to do all the right things in a relationship. I was trying hard not to be like my father and Grandfather. Then one day she says to me out of the blue, this isn't the life I imagined, you're boring and unimaginative. Ouch, that hurt, but truth be known, she had herself a man across town, I assume he was more imaginative and less boring. She told me one year into our relationship that she was fooling around and her new man bought her things and took her places I couldn't afford.

"So what did you do" Mama asked tenderly.

"I thought seriously about going across town and find me a woman who was cheating on her old man and take up with her. Then I thought better of that, I just would not do that to anyone else. Then I thought about looking for love, but knew that if I was patient and waited, I would find someone who loved me just as much as them. Then I thought I would kill her and bury her deep enough in the ground, so the dogs don't get her. But then I found myself a woman who looked just like her, nailed her and dumped her"

I heard mama gasp. Rodney whispered in my ear "damn" I had forgot about Rodney standing on the box next to me. He was so close his cheek touched my ear.

"Just kidding" Mr. Pete said loudly in his booming voice. "I would never do that. I joined the Merchant Marines instead. I went from country to country, port to port and job to job"

I had convinced myself that I was happy being on the sea. I hoped that one day love would come, but if it didn't, I would be fine working on ships around the world. That was until my sister and her husband came to visit me in Japan. My sister and I always kept in touch and her husband is like a brother to me. The whole time they were visiting, he doted over, making sure she was comfortable, he treated her like a queen and she treated him like a king. They were soul mates and very good to each other. Last year they celebrated their thirty-fifth wedding anniversary. At the anniversary I realized that all they had was what I was missing in my life. I missed having someone around. Being there for someone and being needed. A travel companion, a movie mate, someone I could watch the sunrise and sunset with. I know it sounds corny, but it's the truth"

"So" he went on "I retired from the Merchant Marines, went back to church, forgave myself, made peace with my mother before she passed and then I found you. In that order, now I can't lose you, I refuse to lose you and I only want to share my love with you and you alone. And I will not let any man treat you with less than the respect you deserve and I mean that, ex-husband or not"

Mama didn't say a word, I was waiting for her to come back with some crazy argument or yelling, but everything remained quiet. Her uncontrollable sobs let me know that everything was going to be alright. Finally she spoke and told Uncle Pete "old man you don't fight fair, but you know how to get your point across. I love you, baby"

"I love you more" Pete replied

....

Speaking of alright, Rodney was holding me very nicely, like he would never let me go and when I turned to see if he was alright, he kissed me dead on the mouth.

Rodney is going to be with me forever, but he just doesn't know it yet.

....

I asked Grammy a few days later why mama and Mr. Pete were mad at each other and Grammy said "because they in love and don't know how to express it yet"

I told Grammy "if they are in love, why don't they just say it?"

Grammy put her hand on my head and said "listen up child, your mama and Mr. Peter really ain't mad at each other. They just feel each other out. See, your mama ain't never had a real man, you know a man that opens doors and gives you his jacket if it rains or you cold. A man never showed your mama any real attention. Understand? Now this Mr. Pete, he shows your mama attention and he does things for your mama that a man's just supposed to do. Got it?" Grammy looked at me and she could see that I didn't get it. She let out a long sigh.

OK Cola, Kim or whatever the hell you want to be called today. This Mr. Pete is doing all this stuff; all the right things and you ask why don't your mama like it? Because she is a fool and she's used to being treated badly by men like your daddy. Now that she got someone to treat her good, she's waiting for the other shoe to drop. I mean she is waiting for Mr. Pete to treat her bad. Understand?"

Grammy pulled my pigtail and tried to explain to me again."Now your mama boyfriend Mr. Pete, he never been in a relationship with a real woman, he probably been out there with them tramps and floozies. He never had a real woman like your mama and he got feelings for her and now he don't know what to do with them feelings. He a good man, but he been trained not to believe in love. So he makes it like your mama is the problem. He finds himself giving your mama more and more of his heart and it scares the shit out of him.

Grammy asked "why the hell you looking at me like that, don't tell me you still don't understand? OK, one more time and listen close. They both love each other and want to be together, like you and that Rodney boy, always running around giggling and shit, I see y'all. You know the way Rodney makes you feel, well; your mama feels the same way about Mr. Pete. They having sex and things …......

Grammy grabbed my chin and looked me in the eye and said "you in love with that Rodney boy, ain't ya, cause girl he in love with you? You and that Rodney boy ain't having no sex and things are you? You better not let me catch you being nasty"

I tried to turn my head, but Grammy looked me dead in the eye and started laughing "I knew you loved that Rodney boy. Now, your mama and Mr. Pete feel the same way about each other that you and Rodney feel about each other. But unlike you and Rodney, they don't see it yet. They are giving each other something special, something neither had before and once they realize what they have, then they will know what to do, they will get married and all that crap and live happily ever after and blah, blah, blah. Now do you understand?"

"I got it" I shook my head and walked away, but all I really heard Grammy say was that Rodney loved me. I must have been walking on cloud nine because I floated out of the kitchen all the way up to my room.

I'd talk to mama later about why she sent Mr. Pete away. I t better not be because of daddy.

CHAPTER 23

A DOG IN HEAT

"Let it go, it doesn't concern you" Mama said to me.

"I can't let it go mama, I think you owe me an explanation. Why did you let him go? What was your reason and be honest"?

"Oh now you're going to be pig headed, I told you to mind your business and stay in a child's place"

"I guess I got it honest from you" I said to mama as we sat at the table picking greens.

"What are you talking about girl" Mama said to me like she didn't know what we were talking about.

"Your pigheadedness, I got it from you. Because you are being pig headed and foolish. So I am asking you again, why did you send Mr. Pete away? All he did was try to make you happy and you sent him away. Don't you want to ever be happy again in this life?" I asked mama again for the tenth time. If mama thought I was just going to let this one drop, she had another thing coming.

She was going to answer my question. No more beating around the bush.

"Mama, be honest with yourself, Mr. Pete made you the happiest that you have been in years, possibly your life and you know it. Just admit it, say you were happy and I will leave you alone" I knew I was pushing mama to her limit, but at this point I didn't care.

"Happy, you thought Pete made me happy? That man drove me crazy and I just don't need that kind of drama right now. I have a house to maintain and kids to raise. I hardly even knew the man. I don't know what he does when he is away from me. Hell, he could have a wife or another family out there" Mama was talking to me, but continued to stare at the few greens left on the table.

"Mama, how can you sit here and tell stories. You know that Mr. Pete was the most honest man that any of us will ever meet. He is a good man and he treated you well. If you got a little scared, don't worry about it. I am sure he still wants and loves you, just as much as you want and love him" I said as I touched mama's hand and she quickly pulled it away.

"Young lady, I am at my wits end with you. So, why don't you finish with these greens and get out of here"

"Not until you tell me the truth why you pushed Mr. Pete away. You talk about him maybe having someone else. Well maybe the truth is that you have someone else. Maybe you're the one who sneaking and creeping" There, now I said it and no taking it back. I knew I was out of line, but I had to speak my mind.

Mama looked up from the table and I could tell I hit a nerve, but I wasn't going to back away now.

"I'm telling you, you had better check that tone. You better be respectful. I am your mother" She said.

I have never seen my mother this mad. I definitely struck a nerve and now was time for me to go in for the kill. I was just as mad as she was and time I told her a little something about herself.

"Mama, I never thought I would say this, but you need to practice what you preach. You're sitting here trying to say Mr. Pete may be fooling around and running the streets. The truth is that it's you messing around on him. I saw you and daddy the other day. I was putting my bike away in the garage when he jumped over the back fence and knocked on the door. You came out and handed him a beer and you drank your wine as you both sat out there laughing and carrying on. Do you still love him? Did he tell you that he loves you and wants you back? Did you ask him were was his new lady and their children? Did he tell you that he still wants you and loves you? Mama you need to wake up, that man hasn't loved anyone a day in his life"

"Mama yelled what you know about love, you are just a kid. Y u needs to take your ass out of here before you get a whooping. You need to realize that that is your father and maybe he isn't the best, but he has always been there for us whether you know it or not. He is a good man and yes he has done wrong from time to time, but he is a good friend to me. You don't know nothing about love and the heart, maybe one day you will understand love is strange and you cannot walk away from those you care about" Mama was now seething.

To hear her talk good about my father in a good way only got me more riled up. I was beyond pissed. I told her "Really mama, you think daddy wants you back? How can you not see through his game? You are doing well for yourself and you are happy and it is killing him. He comes all the way from across town, creeping over the back fence while your new man is at work to just sit and have a beer with you. You call that love? Mama wake up, the man has a woman and two children across town. What have you always told me and Ty, if a boy ain't good enough to come to the front door and meet your parents, he ain't worth your time. Oh and if a boy don't have manners or doesn't want to be seen with you then he ain't worth a shit. Well mama, I got news for you, the way daddy coming around creeping through the back yard shows that he's a low down dirty dog and ain't worth two shits" There I said it.

Mama stood over me and said "That's enough out of you!"

I said "No it ain't, I'm just starting. Mr. Pete is a real man; he comes to the front door. He takes you out dancing on the weekends. He wines and dines you. He sneaks kisses when he thinks we aren't looking. He treats your children better than their own father ever has. He treats Grammy with much respect and as far as I know he's never cursed you or called you out of your name. What more do you want?"

Mama got real quiet and began to turn. "I don't know what I want. This is eating at me. I have to figure this out. So just leave me alone. Your father is your father. I married him. I took vows. For me that meant something. He wants to come back into our lives. I told him no, but he said he is working on change. He'll do better and I want to believe him and give him a chance"

My mind went black and I lost it on mama. "I can't believe you; you're falling for his bullshit lies again. That is why I hate that bastard, every time something good comes to you, he is right there to fuck it up. He is miserable and he wants you to be miserable. Can you sit here and honestly tell me he wants you back? That hr loves you? Give me a break. He's just a horny dog and when his bitch across town doesn't want him, he turns up here sniffing around like a dog in heat. I hate him I will kill him, I
…......"

Whack, the slap came down hard and fast. It caught me mostly on the cheek. I touched my tongue to my lip and could feel it swell. Mama had hit me with her hand for the first time in my life. I knew I went too far, but at least it got a response from mama. She looked at me and put both hands over her mouth as tears ran from her eyes. She was saying that she was sorry and didn't mean it. She said she lost her temper and was sorry. She had so much on her mind. I touched my cheek and turned to walk away. She told me how right I was about Mr. Pete and how wrong she was about my father. I didn't want to hear any of it. She ran behind me and touched my shoulder, I shrugged her hand away. When I reached the bottom of the step I said "Nothing good ever happens when that man shows his face around here"

120

I felt bad for mama, I felt bad for having pushed her to the limit. My face was stinging from the slap, but I would be alright. I knew that one day we would work through this, but for now she was a fool and it would be a while before I forgave her

CHAPTER 24

GRANNY AND MAMA

I was sitting on the edge of Grammys hospital bed watching her while she slept. The machines around her weren't wheezing, whirling or beeping. I looked from machine to machine, trying to figure out which ones were for monitoring and which machines would keep Grammy alive. Grammy didn't have any tubes up her nose or an oxygen mask on her face, like you see on the hospital television shows. She just lay there, as if she were sleeping. Grammy looked so peaceful and happy; I thought I saw a little smile on her face. I wiped a tear from my eye, then reached down and softly held her hand. I was looking at her hand, studying it, examining it, it was a nice hand. So strong and so warm. I would miss Grammy so much if she died.

Grammy coughed and started to turn over. She now looked restless and agitated. She fought with the covers and then she woke and looked over to me. I smiled and moved the hair away from her face, Grammy smiled back. "Why the hell ain't you in school child?"

"Because it's Saturday Grammy"

"How long have you been watching me sleep?"

"I don't know; I guess about an hour or so"

"You ain't got anything better to do today, than watch me sleep?"

"No, I guess no, not really?"

"OK, then you can watch me sleep if you want" She turned towards the window and started to breathe deeply. I didn't know what to do with myself, so I just sat and watched the covers slowly rise and fall.

Grammy rolled back over quickly and asked "are you really just going to sit there all afternoon and watch me sleep?"

"Yeah I guess so, I don't want to leave you and well Grammy, and I'm scared. I'm scared of you dying; I don't want you to die"

Well baby when your time is up, that's it, gotta go, gotta go. But I ain't going anywhere anytime soon. Why you talking all this dying nonsense.

"You said that you might have cancer. So I was reading about cancer and the paper said that when older people get cancer, the chances are pretty high that they could die from it"

"How old do you think I am?"

"Seventy-two?" was my answer back to her. I looked at Grammy, not knowing what else to say. I never really thought about how old she could be.

Grammy gave me a really strange look and said "seventy-two? Do I look like I'm seventy-two? Girl, you need to go back to counting school. Let's do some math. If you're thirteen years old and your mama had you at twenty, how old does that make your mama?"

I answered "thirty-three" Grammy continued "Now, if I had your mama at twenty-three, how old will that make me?" I thought for a moment and shouted "fifty-six!"

Grammy said "ding" like on the game show, letting me know that I answered correctly.

"Girl 56 is young. My mama, your great grandmother is seventy-eight and she is still alive and can run laps around me.

I said between sobs "But Grammy, I thought when folks get the cancer it kills them?".

Grammy held my face in her hands and tried to explain. "Baby, luckily, I don't have the cancer. I just had some test. The doctors had to check to make sure it wasn't cancer. I just have cyst on my tubes, no cancer and it's not life threatening.

"What would have happened if you had cancer on your tubes?" I wanted to know.

"The doctor said if it was life threatening, I could have had a hysterectomy to take all the cancer out"

"Grammy, what's a hysterectomy?"

"That's when they remove your plumbing" Grammy was patting her belly.

"Huh? Do I have plumbing Grammy?"

"Yes, you have plumbing. Plumbing is what men call our lady parts. These here are your lady parts. You know the baby making factory" Grammy was patting my belly and laughing.

Ain't your mama had the sex talk with you yet? I ain't talking about no damn birds and bees; I'm talking about the differences between a man and a woman. Them things that make a woman special?"

"Yeah kind of, I guess" I was confused.

"Your mama gonna have to tell you about the workings of the lady parts. By the way, where is your mama?"

She took Ty to get shoes for cheer leading. I asked if I could come visit with you. They should be back in a few hours. I wanted to be with you, in case you died.

I ain't dying. You have to live life before you die. Grammy got a whole lot more living to do, good Lord permitting. Tomorrow ain't promised, you could die at any time. That's why your Grammy doesn't hold nothing back. I say what's on my mind, because I would hate to have to die, not saying everything that I wanted to say. When I die, I don't want you crying and making a fuss, you just remember all the good times we had and all that I taught you. I don't want no tears in the end. You just say your goodbyes and live your life the way that I have always taught you. Don't cry for me because I will be in a better place with my Lord. Hell, I may be crying for you, since you will be left here in this world. With all this prejudice and craziness and carrying on. And another thing, don't let them put no tubes in me or keep me alive by no machine. Pull the plug. If God stopped giving me the strength to draw my own breath, then it is time for me to go. Plain and simple, do you understand? Now, no more dying talk, your Grammy will always be here for you.

After our talk, Grammy sent me to the snack room to buy RC colas and moon pies. She told me that I had to sneak them past the nurses' station. She explained that some of the patients were too sick to eat them and we didn't want to tempt them.

The nurses came in to check up on Grammy just as we were about to drink our soda's. The bigger nurse took the sodas and scolded Grammy for having me bring drinks on the floor. After the nurses left we ate our moon pies and laughed.

Grammy and I played checkers and talked the rest of the afternoon until mama showed up. When mama leaned over to give Grammy a hug she said that she smelled chocolate. Mama was furious. "Ma, I know the doctors didn't allow you to eat chocolate, you know better than this. Why did you put Kim up to buying you junk food?"

Grammy laid back in the bed and put on a pitiful look and told mama "Tanya, Kim was just fulfilling a dying old woman's last request. You know I would die if I had to go one more day without a moon pie" Grammy winked at me and I winked back.

Mama told me to say goodbye to Grammy and left the room. I gave Grammy a big hug and said my goodbye. Grammy reached behind her pillow and handed me the empty RC cola can and a moon pie wrapper.

"Thank you for your company and a nice afternoon. I love you baby, you my favorite grandchild. You are always here for me, so I will always be here for you" Grammy said in a kind soft voice.

Grammy pulled me close and gave me another hug and a quick kiss on the cheek.

As I made it to the door and was about to leave, Grammy said "Honey look after my mama and please see if you could pull that stick out her butt, cause that woman don't know how to have fun"

Mama heard Grammy laughing as we made our way to the elevator. Mama asked "So what is so funny that's making your Grammy laugh like that?"

I took a step back and looked at mamas behind. "Grammy told me to see if I could pull that stick out of your butt, but I don't see no stick?"

Mama got mad and grabbed my hand and darn near dragged me to the elevator doors. She mumbled something about Grammy being so darn childish and how she would like to put a stick up Grammy's butt.

CHAPTER 25

I CRIED ALL THE WAY

Mama and Mr. Pete sat in the kitchen talking. Mr. Pete had been back a few days. Mama finally called an apologized and Mr. Pete came right over. I was ecstatic. Now Mama was mad at me for fighting in school. We hadn't spoken to each other in days and I missed her. Now she is at mad at me again and it feels like we will never get back to where we were.

Mr. Pete sat down next to me on the back porch. He held a red Popsicle in the wrapper and with his strong hands broke it in two. He removed the paper and offered me one half of the Popsicle and he took the other half. We sat next to each other for a while in silence, looking out over the back yard. He took a glance at me from the corner of his eye, and then turned back to looking over the freshly mowed lawn.

"Your mama is sittin' in the kitchen and she is hotter than fish grease. She's so mad that she won't even talk to me. I asked her what's wrong and she told me to ask Miss Mohamed Ali. I figured she meant you. So, would you like to tell me what's got your mama's panties in a bunch?" Mr. Pete chuckled and slurped his Popsicle.

"I had a fight at school, but it wasn't my fault. Mama only heard that I got in a fight and she didn't even want to hear why I had to fight"

Mr. Pete put his hand on my shoulder and said "Well, I'm here and I'll listen, if you want to tell me what happened?" He stood and held out his hand "Let's take a walk around the block and you can tell me all about it"

I took his hand and we headed out of the backyard and toward the street. As we walked I was thinking about how nice it would have been if Mr. Pete were my father. He was big, strong and always made me laugh, even when I wasn't in a laughing mood. Now here we were walking hand in hand and he was waiting for me to tell about what happened earlier in the day. As we walked in silence he didn't seem to be in a hurry and he didn't seem to mind that I was still holding his hand. I couldn't remember the last time I held my father's hand or if we ever walked down the street like this. I pushed the thought of my father out of my mind and continued to walk with Mr. Pete.

We were passing the third block when I finally spoke. I didn't know what to say or where to start, so I just started talking. "I guess Mama is really pissed at me for fighting. She was so mad when I came home, that she told me to not say a word and get out of her sight" I looked at Mr. Pete and he didn't say a word, so I kept talking. "It wasn't my fault this time, I swear Mr. Pete, it wasn't. There is this girl in my class and well, she is always getting pushed around by these two boys from another class. The boys call her names and tease her all the time because of her weight and she isn't very pretty. When we came back from spring break, well, her breast have grown, a lot, now the boys are teasing her about her boobs. I told the teachers on the playground that the boys were picking on her and the teachers said that I shouldn't tattle and if Belinda, that's her name, was having trouble, she needs to tell the teachers herself. I asked Belinda why she didn't tell on them and she said that the boys threatened to beat her up if she told and the bigger one slapped her"

I looked at Mr. Pete, he looked upset and his jaw was tight. He stared straight ahead and didn't say a word. So I kept talking.

"Well today I was out on the playground and Belinda was on the swings, so I went and sat next to her. I asked her did she tell anyone what the boys were doing and she said that she was afraid. I was telling her that if she didn't tell, that I would. Just then the boys came up and the taller one Billy told me to mind my business and he called me a crazy bitch. I told them we were going to tell on them for treating Belinda bad. The Shorter one Glen called Belinda fatso and told her that if she told they would slap the shit out of her again. Then he told me that if I told, he would slap the shit out of me. They started teasing Belinda again and Glen put his hand on her breast saying he was going to milk her titty. I told him to get his hand off her and leave her alone. Billy pushed me aside and said that I need to mind my own business. I told him I was going to the teacher and he said if I do, he'll get me after school. He grabbed my chest Mr. Pete and told me to come back when I grow some tits and that's when we got into it"

Mr. Pete finally spoke; he asked "They put their hands on you?"

"Yes and that is when I went off. First I grabbed Billy's finger and twisted it up and to the left, I heard it pop and before he could scream, I punched him in the nose. Then I punched at Glen and missed, and then he slapped me. I gave Glen a front kick to the balls and an elbow to his eye. I back kicked Billy when he started to scream and punched him in the throat. I finished Glen with a round house kick. By the time the teachers came around, both boys were curled up in a ball and crying. Belinda looked at me all surprised and said, "You know karate?" I put my arm around her and whispered in her ear that "yes I know karate and told her that she couldn't tell anyone , not even the teachers. This had to be our secret and no one could find out. If anyone asked, Tell them I hit the boys with a big stick. She smiled a lot and shook her head. Then the teachers took us to the office and called mama"

"You know little girl, I knew you had a lot of fight in you, but damn, I didn't know you could fight. I'm glad that you know how to handle yourself in a bad situation. Where did you learn Karate, your mother never mentioned that"

"My name ain't little girl" I told Mr. Pete, and then I smiled. I winked at him and punched him on the arm. We were still walking hand and hand, blocks away from the house. We turned and headed back towards the house.

"Well, let's see, to make a short story long" I did my best Grammy imitation. "I started karate about five years ago, when I was about eight years old. Michael and his friend Timmy were into Bruce Lee when he was Cato on the Green Hornet TV show. They would watch Bruce Lee kick ass on the show, then after, Michael, Timmy, Ty and me would take sides and play fight.

"Timmy's uncle owns a karate studio and mama signed Michael up for classes. Michael had classes on Saturday morning when mama was at work. So Grammy would take Michael to class. Grammy put me and Ty in classes too, since we had to be there. We told mama we were taking classes, but we just didn't tell how much we were actually learning. Grammy made us all promise not to use karate unless it was for self defense. Michael is a black belt, Ty and I are green belts, we could make black belt next year. Grammy sneaks us out to tournaments. I'm good, but Ty is a little faster and a little better than me in karate, but I can kick her ass in Judo. Did I tell you that we know Judo too?"

Mr. Pete looked at me and said "You never cease to amazing me, you are one hell of a girl"

That made me smile. I asked him to keep the karate and judo a secret because mama would kill Grammy if she found out. Mr. Pete crossed his heart and hoped to die and told me that my secret is safe with him.

Mr. Pete slowed down and looked at me. We were now standing in front of the supermarket where me and Rodney first met him. We went into the store; Mr. Pete bought us Hussmann's potato chips, purple licorice shoestrings, a Tiger Red cream soda pop for me and an orange pop for himself. He had me run back and get windmill cookies for mama, those were her favorites.

We were in the parking lot eating and headed toward the house. Mr. Pete picked up our conversation where we left off. "So you are telling me that all of you kids are trained in martial arts and your mama doesn't know that you all are almost black belts?"

Excuse me, Michael is a black belt, third degree" I said proudly as I chewed on some licorice and took a sip of pop.

Mr. Pete looked at me, laughed and shook his head. He said "Amazing, I'm speechless and I really don't know what to say. You are truly an interesting young lady. Is there anything else I need to know about you?"

"Well, I like to draw; I am at the best in my art class. I'm the fastest kid in my school and one day I plan to be in the FBI or CIA. My favorite food is ribs, favorite drink is Tiger red cream soda and some days I crave White Castles. One day I plan on marrying Rodney, but he just doesn't know it yet. When he realizes that he loves me and just can't live without me, he's going to ask me to marry him. When that happens, I will let him think it was his idea. So, now that I told you about me, what about you?"

Mr. Pete went on to tell me about himself, he also knew martial arts, his favorite food was turkey, he could draw and he wrote a couple of books about traveling the world. He also confided in me that in the short time that he has known my mama, he found her to be amazing and he is falling for her. He then paused when we got to the sidewalk in front of our house and told me that he loved mama. I smiled wide and was ready to scream when he told me that I have to keep it a secret for a while. He told me how this was all new to him and he didn't want to rush into anything too soon with mama. He confessed that this is the first time that he has ever been in love like this and he was a little scared.

I told him that I felt the same about Rodney and that I understood where he was coming from. I also told him that it was alright if he and mama had sex. Grammy tells mama all the time that it's been many a month on Sunday since she last had any. Grammy says if she don't get some soon that thing gonna close up like a clam and no man will ever be able to get inside. Use it lose it Grammy says to mama all of the time. I figure you can help mama use it so she don't lose it.

Mr. Pete choked and sprayed orange pop out his nose. I guess he must have drunk too fast and it went down the wrong pipe. I do that sometimes myself.

....

When we made it in the house, mama was waiting for us. She was upset when she saw we had pops, chips and candy. She said "Pete we don't reward these kids for fighting …." Mama stopped talking when he handed her the windmill cookies and gave her a big smile. Mama looked at him and frowned, she took the cookies and one corner of her mouth went up in a half smile. Mr. Pete was learning well. I told him that windmill cookies were mamas favorite and if he was ever in trouble bring her home windmill cookies.

Mr. Pete looked at mama and said "we all need to talk, seems Kim was trying to do the right thing and tell the teachers, but …..." Mama waved her hands in the air and told Mr. Pete to stop right there. She said that the school had called while we were out. The boys confessed to bullying and putting their hands on Belinda and Kim. The boys were suspended and Kim can return to school in the morning, but will have to write an essay about fighting at school.

"Now, where have you two been all this time, I hope you left room for dinner. The rest of us have eaten" Mama opened her bag of cookies, took one out and took a bite. She pointed a cookie at me and Mr. Pete and said "After the two of you eat, you can wash all them dinner dishes. Seeing how you two have bonded, you can continue to bond over them suds. That is part of your punishment for eating junk food before dinner. When you two get done, Kim, you go upstairs, get ready for school and get your butt in the bed early. Pete, you come in the living room and bring them strong hand, my neck is stiff and I need a massage"

Me and Mr. Pete said "yes ma'am" in unison as mama left the kitchen. I went to the cupboard and grabbed our plates, while he got the silverware and drinks. I talked about school and Rodney. He talked about work and mama. We told each other jokes and played while we did dishes. When we finished we went into the living room, I gave mama a big hug and a kiss and thanked her. I turned to Mr. Pete, gave him a big hug and thanked him. He hugged me back and thanked me too and I asked why he was thanking me, I didn't do anything. He said thank you for letting me get to know you.

I said you're welcome and told him to take care of mama. Then I ran up the stairs.

I ran to Ty's room and sat on her bed and told her about my walk with Mr. Pete and how we bonded. I told her about everything except him loving mama. That was something he could tell Ty when it was their time to bond.

I told Ty how I let Mr. Pete know that it was alright for him to have sex with mama. I let Ty know that it would be best for mama, because like Grammy said "she had to use it or lose it"

Ty asked me if I thought mama would let Mr. Pete use 'it' so she doesn't lose it. I told her that I hoped she would, because whatever 'it' is, Grammy said once mama gave 'it' away, she would be feel good and be much happier.

Ty and I agreed that we wanted mama to be happy. Then we both wished we knew what 'it' was and wondered if we had it too, so we give 'it' away.

CHAPTER 26

HE MISSES ME LIKE CRAZY

I opened my bedroom curtain to dark gray streaked skies. I stared for a moment at the Saturday morning gloom and sighed. The rain was coming down as a hard steady drizzle. The leaves in the trees were soaked and wilted. They were dreary shades of browns, yellows and reds.

I hugged my favorite teddy bear and sighed out loud. I tossed him in the air a few times, then kicked him towards the toy box. I jumped on my bed and began to bounce up and down like I was on a trampoline. I heard Mama yell from the kitchen, telling me to stop bouncing on the bed. I bounced a few more times than plopped down on my butt. I rolled on my back with my head hanging off the bed staring at the ceiling. I bouncing a ball off the wall until mama yelled for me to stop.

I picked up a box of tissue sitting on the dresser and blew my nose. I threw the tissue in the trash and tossed the box onto the floor. I was bored to tears and I didn't know what to do with myself.

I walked into the kitchen and mama was sitting at the table, drinking coffee and skimming through a magazine. She was rubbing her neck and slowly pushing the pages.

"Hey mama, what are you doing?" I asked.

Mama lifted her head and shrugged her shoulders and said "nothing much, what are you up to besides destroying your room?"

I replied in a nonchalant tone "nothing much, do you want to play a game?"

Mama looked at me then scrunched up her face and said "naw, do you want to bake something?"

"Naw" I said back to mama "do you want to watch television, Soul Train is on?"

"Naw" mama said as she reached for me, I sat on her lap and she put her chin on my head and wrapped an arm around my shoulders. "This is the first time that you've been by yourself in a while. I guess you're kinda lonely without your sister and Rodney around? You really miss them, huh?"

"Yeah mama, I guess I do miss them a little" I was talking to mama in a squeaky little voice that didn't sound like mine. "I guess you're missing Mr. Pete, huh?"

"Yes, baby I am. Mama said quietly and kissed me on the head "I am missing him like crazy. I can't remember ever missing someone like this in my life. I was just wondering how can I care so much for a man that I just met a few weeks ago. Sometimes it feels like I have known him my whole life"

"I know what you mean mama; this is the first time that I haven't been around Rodney since I met him a few months ago. I think that he has really grown on me, you know, somehow he got under my skin" I was saying while I looked into mama's eyes and she smiled.

"Men" mama said as she patted me on my back, telling me to stand up. She made her way to the freezer and grabbed a twin orange Popsicle and broke it in two. She handed me half and she kept the other half for herself.

"Mama, is it alright that the only friend that I have is Rodney? Should I have more girl friends or get to know other guys? I know it sounds crazy, but I have a lot of fun with Rodney and we have a lot in common. Rodney treats me really nice. He walks me to and from school every day. Sometimes he will bring me a pop and candy for no reason" I took a big bite of my Popsicle.

Mama was now seated across from me at the kitchen table studying me. You know, staring at me like I was an alien.

"Who are you and what did you do with my daughter?" Mama asked as she touched my cheek.

Mama smiled softly and said "Baby, in this world you only get two true friends. It is nice that you found a friend in Rodney. It warms my heart that he treats you so nice. The two of you should just enjoy each other's company for the time being. By the way, where is he today?"

"Rodney went to Cleveland with his father to visit family. He won't be back until late Sunday night. He told me that if his father will let him, he would call me sometime today and sometime after church tomorrow"

"So is that why you decided not to sleep over at Regina's house with Ty, because you were waiting on Rodney's call?" mama asked.

"No mama, I don't think so. I mean Regina is cool and all, but she is Ty's friend. I know that sometimes they want to do things together without me hanging around. So I decide to let them have some space. Anyway Regina is always talking, laughing and clowning. I just wasn't in the mood for her today"

"I understand, I love that child to death, but sometimes she gets to be a handful" Mama talked while she made her way back to the freezer to get us a second Popsicle. She held up a cherry and a grape. I pointed to grape and mama broke it into two and handed me half and she took the other half. She sat across from me and asked "What do you think about Mr. Pete?"

"I like him mama, I liked him from the very start. He is a very nice man and he treats you very nice. Is he your soul mate? Do you love him? I think he fell in love with you at first sight. Will you marry him if he asks you?" I was talking a mile a minute and was about to ask a few more question, when I noticed mama's cheeks were red and she had a dreamy look in her eyes. "You love him don't you?" I screamed and clapped my hands.

Mama looked down at the table and mumbled "yes, I do!" then she looked up at me blushing and said "I love this man and I miss him when he's gone and I want our time together to last forever. He is good to my children and he respects my mama. He even jokes with Grammy, he calls her a queen. He told Grammy that I was his princess, so Grammy had to be a queen. That was the first time that I have seen your Grammy speechless. You have to love any man that can leave your Grammy speechless"

"I guess we are a couple of lucky girls with a couple very special boys in our life"

I shook my head as I agreed with mama "So, where is Mr. Pete today?"

"He went to Tennessee with his cousin to see about some land that his grandmother left them. He should be back Monday afternoon or Tuesday morning. He's already called me twice today, once while he was on the road and the other to let me know they made it. I can't remember your father ever checking in with me or making sure that I alright. This is new for me and you know what, it feels good. I knew that I always had to take care of you, your sister and your brother, but it feels good to finally have someone take care of me"

Mama gathered up the wrappers and the Popsicle sticks and walked over to the garbage can. She lifted the lid and tossed the garbage. She grabbed a dish cloth and wiped the table, I watched.

"Mama, you know Rodney thinks the world of you. He said that if it weren't for our family, he would probably sit at home all day and cry for his mother. He said he thinks of you as his second mother, you know, since you and his mother were best friends. I'm sure she would be happy knowing that you are here for him"

Rodney father wanted me to tell you that they can't thank you enough for helping them get through their rough time" Mama leaned on the counter and put her fist to her mouth and let a tear drop roll down her cheek.

I walked over to mama and we stood there for the longest time and hugged each other. We didn't speak or move until the phone rang and gave us both a jolt. Mama slowly reached over and lifted the phone gently off the cradle and in her low sultry voice said "hello" followed by a few um huhs and couple of that's nice baby and finally, I miss you too, baby. I thought that is so nice that mama has someone who cares enough to call her when they were away. Mama has been so happy lately, I just wish that I could be that happy.

Then mama put the phone to my ear and said "it's for you Kim, its Rodney"

....

By the time I got off the phone with Rodney, I was on cloud nine. It was like I was on speed or some new type of drug. We were both talking so fast, that we were talking over each other, I don't know if either of us got to finish a sentence. I filled him in on my morning and he told me about the ride to Cleveland and how they stopped at an Amish village on the way. He told me that he got me four different types of licorice and a few wooden toys. He told me again that he would be home Sunday evening. He then told me he would call tomorrow and before he hung up, he told me that he missed me like crazy.

I must have stood there for a few minutes listening to the dial tone with my mouth wide open because mama asked if Rodney was still on the line and all I could do was hand her the phone. She asked if everything was alright and all I could say was "he misses me like crazy"

CHAPTER 27

CAN I HAVE YOUR BLESSINGS

We were sitting on the porch, we being, Michael, Ty, Rodney, Regina and myself. We had just returned from the store. Michael bought a big bag of treats for everyone to share. We had garlic dill pickles, penny candy, potato chips, cookies and my favorite Tiger Red cream soda.

Michael was telling us stories of what it was like living with Uncle Len on his big farm outside of Columbus, Georgia. He described the sky; he said it was so blue during the day and pitch black at night with millions of stars. The way Michael described the sky made me feel like I was there. I asked him "Michael were there more stars than what we see at the planetarium here in Cincinnati?" He said it was just as many or even more. He told us that whenever there was a full moon, the moon was so big and shined so bright that it looked like it was sitting at the edge of the cornfield.

He told us how black people and white people treated each other differently down south. Even though it was the seventies, black people still had to watch what they said around white people and the places they traveled to. Some towns had signs that warned "nigger, don't let the sun go down on your black ass"

Michael also told us about the good parts of the south that he had seen with his new friends. He said for the most part everyone was friendly and they love to have a good time. He said when he first moved there everyone called him a Yankee or the boy from up north. They used to laugh at his funny northern accent and he would laugh at their southern drawl.

He noticed that once everyone got used to his accent and him being from the north, they treated him like family. Where ever he went, someone would offer to cook him a good meal or invite him to a picnic or party. They would look out for him because he was Lem's people. Michael was smiling so big when he talked about the south that I think he missed being there.

Rodney asked Michael how the southern girls are and if they are finer and nicer than the northern girls. I gave Rodney a stern look and a bop on the head. Michael smiled and said that the women down south were all sugar and spice and everything nice with their thick southern drawl and big corn fed booties. Michael and Rodney slapped each other five and chuckled like a couple of perverts. Regina stood and said "ain't no women finer than the ones in Cincinnati and y'all know it, why you playing'" Just look at us, we fine as hell and we have booties too. Us girls got up and started walking sexy and sticking out our butts.

"Look at them fine ladies" Mr. Pete said as he walked toward the steps laughing.

"Hey Mr. Pete" we all said in unison as he came upon the porch.

"Mr. Pete, are the girls in the south finer than the girls in the north?" Regina asked, putting Mr. Pete on the spot.

"That's a tough question Regina, let me think. To me all women are beautiful, regardless of where they come from. I think a woman can be fine as all get out, but if she has a funky attitude, that will make her ugly. And if a woman who may not be so fine has a great attitude, then that will make her beautiful" Mr. Pete smiled and looked at Michael and said "sounds to me like you may have found you a little lady in the south that's got your nose open?"

Michael smiled "Well, if having my nose open means that I found a lady that I like, then, yes sir, I found a lady who has my nose wide open"

We all looked at Michael surprised. This was the first time we ever heard of Michael liking someone. He never brought a girl around the house that he would call his girlfriend.

"Michael, I thought you were waiting for me, you know that I'm the only woman for you" Regina joked.

"Regina you cool, but you're like a little sister to me, I found me a lady that is a lady. Here take a look at her picture" He showed a picture to us all of a really beautiful girl. "Gorgeous isn't she. Next time I come up here I am going to bring her to meet mama. I know mama will like her, because my girl is the bomb"

Ty walked over to Michael and gave him a big hug and said "aw, my big brother is in love, that's so cute" Then we all started teasing him.

"Alright y'all give Michael a break" Mr. Pete stood laughing and put his hands on Michael's shoulders. I think it's nice that he found someone special. Speaking of someone special, where is your mama?"

"She's in the basement Mr. Pete, washing clothes, do you want me to get her?" I started toward the door.

"No, not yet, I'm glad you all are here. I was wondering if you all would like to join me in a walk to your Grammy's house. There is something I want to ask her and I would like all of you to be there. I also want you all to be a witness, just in case Grammy doesn't like what I ask her and she tries to beat me up. He gave us a smile and a wink, then told me to go tell mama that we were all going to Grammy's for a few.

I opened the door and yelled "mama, we are going to Grammy's and well, be back in a little while, OK" mama yelled back and told us to be back by dinner and to lock the door. I yelled back "OK" then looked at Mr. Pete and said "mama said OK, let's go" and I led the group in our walk to Grammy's house.

. . . .

When we got to Grammy's house, she was sitting on the front porch talking on the phone with a beer on the table next to her. Grammy held up her index finger, wanting us to give her a moment. Mr. Pete sat in a chair while the rest of us sat on the banister. When Grammy finished her call she took a sip of beer and asked us why everyone was on her porch.

Mr. Pete turned toward Grammy and said "they are all here because of me. I wanted to ask you a question and I thought it would be nice if they were along to hear your answer."

Grammy looked at Mr. Pete over the top of her glass and when she finished drinking and put the glass on the table, she told him "go on"

He said "Grammy, I mean Ms. Johnson, I would like to see as much of your daughter as possible. I would like to be a part of her life. I know that we haven't known each other long, but I love her. I love her so much that I would like to ask your blessings to marry Tanya" He then looked to each of us and said "I would like to ask for all of your blessings"

It must have taken a few minutes for what he said to register with all of us, because no one said a word. Then Michael asked "are you asking to marry our mother?" as a smile started to cover his face.

Then Grammy looked at Mr. Pete and said "You know son, you didn't have to ask for my blessings, y'all old enough to just go jump the broom. But since you were considerate enough to think about asking, then yes, son, you have my blessing. Mr. Pete stood up and then took Grammy's hand and then gave her a hug. Grammy said "OK, you have my blessing. son. So, from this day forward, you gonna have to call me mom" Mr. Pete looked at her and said "OK, mom"

He turned to us kids and said "Now, you all, I would like to ask you for your blessings to marry your mother. I know that she went through a lot with your father, but I'm not your father. I am just Mr. Pete and I would like to promise to you all that I would love your mother and treat her right until my dying days. I would like to be a part of all of your lives"

What do you think he asked, he put out his arms and we all went in for a hug, even the boys. We told him that we would accept him into our family.

He wanted to do a big proposal to mama with all if there at the diner, the first place that he laid eyes on her.

....

We were all inside the diner when Mr. Pete and mama came in. They were talking to the waitress. It was the same waitress that was there when Mr. Pete bought us lunch. She grabbed a couple of menus and walked them back to the back. The first person mama saw was Mr. Price, Rodney's father. He greeted her and they hugged. As they made it to the back she saw the rest of us sitting in the big booth. She looked at all of us and said "OK, what's going on here?" We all just smiled and laughed.

She turned to Mr. Pete and he held her hand and went down on one knee. Mr. Price opened up a little box and Mr. Pete took the ring that was inside. Everything seemed to go in slow motion. It took a moment for mama to realize what was happening.

Mr. Pete started his proposal "Tanya, I have always been in love with the thought of being in love, but I have never truly loved anyone until I met you. After being with you, talking with, sharing with you, I knew that yours was the love that I have always dreamed about. The love I showed to you and the love you showed me is real and I can't go another day without us belonging to each other. Tanya will you marry me. A single tear ran down mama's cheek, she looked deep into Mr. Pete's eyes, then looked at us and we all said "yes" then mama looked back at Mr. Pete and shook her head up and down "yes" she said and then embraced him. Mama was crying hard, she was crying so hard that she was boo hooing. We all cried, the customers and the waitresses were crying too. It was very emotional.

Mama looked at all of us and said "I guess you all knew?"

Grammy said "yes, this young man came by my house the other day and asked us all for our blessing. I told you Tanya, this is a good man that cares the world for you. Shit, if you didn't say yes, I was going to take him for myself. You're lucky he saw you first"

Laughter erupted and everyone in the place was congratulating them and making a fuss. Mama was so happy

CHAPTER 28

LET THE PARTY BEGIN

Grammy surprised mama with a bachelorette party at her house. She ordered in pizza, stayed up late watching old movies and we listened to mama tell us all about her dress, the romantic honeymoon that her and Mr. Pete had planned in Acapulco, how nervous she was about flying and how she'll miss us during her honeymoon. Mama said she was excited to get on a plane, she has never flown

The men had a bachelor party.

....

Mama and Mr. Pete were married in our backyard on the first day of spring. Mama told Mr. Pete that he could pick the date, but she was going to take care of everything else. He chose the first day of spring, he said that it was a good start to a new beginning.

....

The ceremony was beautiful and it was mainly family and close friends. The grooms party consisted of the best man who was Mr. Pete's father. The groomsmen were Uncle Lem, my brother Michael and Rodney. The brides party consisted of Grammy who was mama's maid of honor, Regina, Ty and me were mama's bride's maids. Mama said that she wanted all of her girls and boys to take part in her special day.

Mr. Pete wore a white tux with a light blue cummerbund, top hat and tails. The rest of the men had light blue tux with a white cummerbund. They looked like the Temptations getting ready to put on a show.

Mama wore a light canary yellow dress with yellow flowers in her hair, she was gorgeous. Grammy wore a pink mini skirt, a white puffed sleeve shirt and white go boots, the rest of us wore pink skirts and white blouses.

The ceremony went perfectly. Mr. Pete was so nervous that he had to read his vows from index cards because he couldn't remember what he wrote. He said nice things about mama and promised to love her always and he had a few jokes thrown in. Mama's vows were funny and light also, instead of until death do we part, she said "there is no way in hell that I would ever leave this man's side and no way in hell he'll be leaving mine. I waited too long for someone this good to come along and love me for me and I am not giving it up without a fight, not in this life or the next life. So instead of until death do we part, let's say until the end of this life, then over the threshold into the next life and beyond, we WILL be together hand in hand and heart to heart, because I will never let you go Peterson Alvin Mitchell.

After the I do's were said and they jumped the broom, the newlyweds and the wedding party lined up for pictures. Mama and Mr. Pete took a ton of pictures, first by themselves as bride and groom, then with the wedding party and finally taking group pictures with all that came to share their special day. The receiving line was nice, we got to meet all of Mr. Pete's family and friends. His parents were so nice and his sister and brother in law, who currently lived in Amsterdam, were dressed so elegantly that you would think that they were royalty. Mr. Pete's sister was just as tall as mama, her skin was flawless and she was the color of dark chocolate candy with the whitest teeth I ever saw, she looked like she could be a princess of an African country.

The reception started out with a wonderful meal catered by the very restaurant where Mr. Pete first laid eyes on mama. He told the story of how he saw mama sitting at the table with her daughters and how for the first time in his life, he saw what he was missing, a family of his own.

At the time he didn't know that mama was the woman that he would be settling down with. He just felt it would be nice to treat a beautiful woman and her lovely family to lunch. His plans were a quick trip here to his hometown of Cincinnati to sell some property left to him by his Aunt and Uncle then move on to Los Angeles or New York. But after a few days of living in his Aunts house, he realized that he just couldn't bring himself to sell the old place. He let a cousin stay in his Aunts place while he went back to Dallas and planned his move to either the east or west coast. As he packed his belongings, he couldn't stop thinking about the woman in the restaurant. For the first time in his life, he realized that he was all alone and living out of a suitcase was getting old. He came back to Cincinnati not sure if he would ever see the woman in the diner again or if she was married or even wanted to be bothered with him. He then told of the day Rodney and I saw him in the store and how I told him that he was meant to be with mama. He was so happy that I had found him and I set up the meeting between he and mama.

So he went to Dallas and moved all his belongings here, where he would. The more he drove around town, the more he knew that this was the place he was meant to be.

He and mama told the story of their first almost meeting in Newton's restaurant.

CHAPTER 29

REALLY

Yesterday was a rough day for everyone. Uncle Len had us clean the house from top to bottom. He said we needed to clean up this pig sty before mama and Daddy Pete's return. Did you catch that? I called him daddy Pete instead of Mr. Pete. I figured since he and mama are now married, it would be nice to call him daddy Pete. I'll spring out daddy Pete when they return. Anyway, yesterday Uncle Len worked our butts off.

It started after breakfast. Uncle Len stood up and put his hands behind his back like a drill instructor would. He didn't say a word, just looked around the messy house. Uh oh, I've seen this look before Grammy whispered to me as she made her way to the basement door. Uncle Len is a retired Army drill instructor and now he was in Army drill instructor mode. He knocked four times hard on the table to get everyone's attention. Once everyone was quiet Uncle Len stood tall and looked at each one of us. He said "I hope you all enjoyed the chow, now it's time to get to work. Go change into your work clothes and report back to the kitchen in twenty minutes for duty." We all looked at him like he was crazy.

He laughed as he spoke "I guess you all thought that was a request? Well, it wasn't, it was an order. When you return I will assign chores and teams. I expect this house to be spotless before noon."

He looked at his watch and said "you all now have nineteen minutes. I suggest you maggots get a move on. You ate my food and drank my drink, now you're going to work it off. That includes everyone, Rodney, Regina and you too Mr. Price." He was now smiling and pointing at Rodney's father. Everyone laughed.

Rodney's father stood and saluted.

When we returned to the kitchen Uncle Len split us up into teams and gave us each a part of the house to clean. He and Grammy cleaned the kitchen and mopped the floors. Rodney's father and my brother Michael did the yard work and took care of everything outside. Rodney and I took care of the living room, dining room and the first floor. Ty and Regina got the bedrooms, bathrooms and second floor.

Uncle Len came around from time to time to inspect our areas to make sure we were making progress. He called us maggots and told us there would be no chow until the job was done to his liking.

After all the chores were done we all met back in the kitchen. Everyone stood around waiting for Uncle Len to finish his inspection of the house. We were still holding buckets and dirty rags. There was stew cooking on the stove and I think I heard everyone's stomach growling. I doubt any of us had worked this hard in a long time. We were dirty, sweaty and tired. Uncle Len came in the kitchen looked at us and gave two thumbs up. Everyone relaxed. Some of us were pulling out chairs while the rest were headed to the cabinet for bowls.

"Hell no!" Uncle Len shouted. "No food until everyone cleans up. Everyone eats outside on the picnic table. You maggots are not messing up my kitchen. You have twenty minutes until chow time; I suggest you go clean up."

Everyone agreed to meet back in twenty minutes. Rodney, his father and Regina were headed for the front door, making their way home. Michael was on his way up the steps with Ty right behind. Uncle Len made his way out the back door. I was standing alone in the kitchen.

I heard the door to the basement open slowly and Grammy peaked out. "Are they all gone?" she asked in a whisper.

I nodded yes as Grammy quietly made her way into the kitchen. I watched as she tip toed over to the cabinet and got two coffee cups. She then reached in the drawer and got two spoons. She handed me the spoons as she removed the lid from the pot and set it quietly on the stove. She did a quick stir and filled the two coffee cups with stew. She handed me one of the cups as she put the lid back on the pot. She took a slice of cornbread from the skillet and put it on a piece of towel paper. Somehow Grammy balanced the stew and cornbread as reached over and grabbed four cookies and a soda. I stood and watched in amazement. She bumped me with her hip, moving me toward the basement door. I grabbed myself a soda as we quickly made our way down the basement steps.

....

Grammy and I finished our snack. We used the downstairs bathroom to wash up. We changed into two pairs of mama's clean sweats from the laundry. Mama's sweats were way too big for both of us. We laughed at how silly we both looked. Grammy put a finger to her lips as we quietly made our way up to the kitchen. I was look out while Grammy quickly washed, dried and returned the cups to the cabinet and the spoons to the drawer. We then headed to the living room and waited for the others to arrive.

First to arrive was Regina and she brought her parents. They had a pineapple, a big bowl of fruit and a bottle of rum. Rodney and his father came shortly after. Michael and Ty made their way down the stairs a few minutes later. Uncle Len was last making his way in from the garage.

The festivities were about to begin. Michael and Uncle Len had put down table cloths and set up extra chairs. Grammy ladled stew into bowls as everyone made their way through the chow line. Regina and Ty poured the drinks and Regina handed them out as everyone made their way to the back yard. We were all seated and settled in at the picnic tables. Mr. Price blessed the food and prayed for a safe return for mama and daddy Pete. Everyone said Amen and we attacked the food like vultures.

Regina's parents made rum punch for the adults and a delicious pineapple drink for the kids. Regina's parents were immigrants originally from the Islands mama and daddy Pete were honeymooning on. Their eyes lit up as they told us all about the beauty and the history of their island. Regina's mother mentioned that mama and daddy Pete was the dinner guest at her parents' house a few times during their stay. Regina's father spoke with a booming voice and heavy accent. He told jokes and sang some songs from his island.

We ate, drank, talked and laughed until it was almost dark. I think everyone forgot about how hard we worked that afternoon. It felt good, but to be honest, I wished mama were here. I missed her so much and couldn't wait for her to come home. Funny thing was I missed daddy Pete too. He was such a nice man.

....

Mama and Mr. Pete were due home in two days. The house was to be decorated and the stage was set for a huge welcome home party. Uncle Len and Michael had painted a huge banner to put above the front porch. Rodney and I were decorated the inside of the house. Ty and Regina planned the meal and fussed over which desserts to make. Grammy, being Grammy looked on while drinking the rum that Regina's parents left the night before.

The phone rang and everyone seemed to freeze.

Grammy, who was sitting closest to the phone, yelled "I got it, you all back off, I got the damn phone" She finally answered on the fourth ring.

We all laughed as she picked up the receiver and tried to talk into the ear piece instead of the mouth piece.

She slurred into the receiver "hello, state your name and business" She paused for a moment then said "no, Tanya ain't here, she's on her honeymoon. What, oh, this is Tanya. Hey daughter of mine, how the hell are you doing?"

Ty yelled "hey everyone mama is on the phone" Uncle Len and Michael came into the kitchen from the back porch. We all sat down at the kitchen table.

Grammy was shushing everyone; she said that she couldn't hear. Grammy asked mama about the island she was on, how she was being treated by the islanders and if she had seen Billy Dee Williams or Diana Ross. Grammy let out a big laugh and told everyone that mama saw Gladys Knight on the plane and got her picture and autograph. Grammy relayed everything that mama was telling her over the phone. Grammy told us how daddy Pete took mama snorkeling and how they swam with the dolphins. At one point Grammy had to tell mama to slow down, because she was talking a mile a minute.

After a few minutes of talking, Grammy passed the phone to Michael. Michael in turn passed the phone to Ty so she could speak, then on to me.

When I said my goodbyes to mama, I held the phone out to Regina and told her that mama has something to tell her.

Regina took the phone and after a moment of listening her face lit up like the fourth of July. She must have said "really" about twenty times. She then told mama all about our big welcome home surprise, not realizing that she had gave away the whole surprise. No one seemed to care and it really didn't matter, we were just ready for mama to come home. At the end of her conversation, she told mama she loved her, to say hello to her Grandparents and to hurry home. Then she pushed the phone at Rodney.

Regina looked to Ty and said "Ms. N said my grandmother bought her a beautiful locket and she gave us matching lockets also." Then they both screamed with excitement.

Rodney took the phone from Regina and turned his back to us, so he could hear. Uncle Lem and Michael went out on the back porch. Regina and Ty took few cookies out of the jar and left the room laughing. Grammy poured another glass of rum and headed to the back porch. I was now alone with Rodney in the kitchen. I held his hand while he talked to mama. He tilted the phone so I could listen in on their conversation, we were cheek to cheek. I heard mama on the other end of the phone tell Rodney to look out for me. Rodney told her she couldn't pay him enough, and then he laughed and promised that he would try. I wondered what all that was about, but it felt good to hear him tell mama he would look out for me.

Before Rodney got off the phone with mama he told her that he loved her, just as much as he loved his own mother. Then to lighten the mood, Rodney told mama a funny joke about a guy named Artie and how Artie choked three for a dollar at Kroger. It was a corny joke, but we laughed and so did mama. I was still cheek to cheek with Rodney as we held the receiver so we both could hear and said our goodbyes to mama.

I thought of mama and Mr. Pete riding through the mountains on a scooter. Wind in their hair and the ocean and beaches in full view. Regina's mother described it so vividly I felt like I was there.

Then I thought of me and Rodney on a beach on an island. I seemed to daydream about him a lot lately. When I looked down, Rodney and I were still holding hands and standing very close to each other. We were smiling at each other when Rodney kissed me on the cheek and I kissed his cheek. Then I turned and our lips met for a second just as the phone buzzed and the operator said "if you would like to make a call, please hang up and try again" We giggled as we hung the receiver back on the wall unit. We looked at each other again and we were going to go back in for another smooch when I heard Ty and Regina giggling. Grammy chimed in "don't stop on account of us"

Rodney and I turned to see that Grammy, Regina, Ty, Michael and Uncle Len were there to witness our first kiss. I was so embarrassed, but the kiss felt so good and so right, that I kissed Rodney again, smack dab on the lips in front of everyone.

Now, I bet they didn't see that one coming!

CHAPTER 30

HONEYMOON TIME

Sunday morning shortly before sunrise Tanya was in the middle of a nice dream when she felt something binding her legs together. She tried to twist to set herself free, but with no luck. Each time she moved the binding became tighter. She reached down with her hands and felt the soft silky fabric and her first thought was a giant spider web, could she be in a spider web? She lay still for a moment, not sure what to do. She slowly opened her eyes and could only see grass above her. She looked to her left and out of an open window and could only make out specks of light. Next to her, she felt something warm. It was moving slightly and had a low growl. Was this the spider ready to devour her? If it was, she wasn't going down without a fight.

She steadied herself and came up with a plan. She would roll to her right and pin the spider down with her body. She would then yell for her son Michael and the girls for help. She started with a countdown three, two …. Then the spider moved and she attacked. She rolled on top of the spider quickly and was able to put both arms around him. He didn't put up much of a fight. She moved her legs and was able to get the left one free. She was now on top with legs and arm tying the spider up. She was ready to yell for help from the kids when she noticed that this wasn't a spider, it was a man. She must have been dreaming. She was half awake, but groggy and wondered what a man was doing in her bed. She looked around, this wasn't her room. Looking down on the man, he was smiling up at her. Then it all came to her as she fully awoke. She was no longer alone and this was no big spider in her bed, it was her husband and they are on their honeymoon.

She laughed and hugged him tightly. She held on like she would never let go. It had been years since she woke up next to a man and the first time she woke up on top. She laughed as she thought about the spider dream. The hunter was now the prey and she had her man pinned down and she would never let him go.

Looking up at his bride Peter Mitchell couldn't help but smile. It felt so good to wake up to the woman he loved holding him so tight. This was something he could get used to. As she lay on top of him squeezing, he knew that she truly loved him, as much as he loved her. He never had a chance to tell her how alone he had been for so many years until he met her. Somehow he figured she could sense his loneliness, just like he sensed hers. He was happy that they found each other. Well actually it was Kim that found him and put the two of them together. He owed Kim big time.

The newlyweds lay together for hours. Tanya was on top, Pete on the bottom. They looked out of the open window as lights slowly came on from the village below. They were both feeling melancholy about the day ahead. This was their last morning on the island. The past few days were a blur as Tonya and Pete participated in everything that paradise had to offer. Everything for Tanya was a first. They enjoyed snorkeling, hang gliding, jet skis and the crazy banana boat. She took swim classes in high school and college, but was never much for water. Pete, a strong swimmer, was so patient and attentive that he made it all fun for Tanya. As they lay in silence, the two realized that it was nice to have someone to share new adventures with. From this day forward, each day would be a new adventure together.

The lovers looked deeply into each other's eyes. Tanya broke the silence. "Honey, if there was anything that you could do right now, what would it be?"

An evil grin crossed his face "besides making love to you? I guess people watching at that beach side hut with the fresh fruit and pineapple rum. The place we had brunch a few days ago"

She smiled and kissed his shoulder. "I remember, the owner was so nice to us, he let us sample each dish he made. I thought you were going to have to roll me out of there. Oh, he did tell us that if we liked his brunch, that we would love his breakfast. We should go there for breakfast and take him and his lovely wife a gift"

He thought for a moment "Great idea babe! We could take off as soon as the sun comes up"

She was quiet for a moment, and then suggested "These sunrises and sunsets are magnificent. Why not take off now and we can catch the sunrise on the beach. We can make love to the sun rising on our final day in paradise"

He nodded his head "That would be great!" She was still lying on top of him holding him tightly. He asks her. "Hey, by the way, are you going to wrap me up like this every morning, I really like this?"

She gave an evil laugh and said "Oh yeah, there will plenty of mornings like this, but we'll need to get a set of these silk sheets so you can entangle me in your web"

He wasn't sure what she was talking about, but if it's silk sheets his baby wanted, then silk sheets his baby will have!

....

Tanya and Pete were sitting on the scooter shortly before dawn. They did a final check for their sunrise excursion. Beach blanket in left basket and fine bottle of champagne they received from the resort they were staying in the right. They figured it would be a nice to re-gift the champagne to the nice couple at the hut where they planned to have breakfast.

Looking over the horizon they could see a sliver of pink. They figured they had better get a move on to catch the suns first light. Heading toward the beach there was an ample amount of foot traffic and few scooters on the road. Tanya smiled, Rush hour on the island. This was a typical work day for the islanders. Tanya feeling the warm breeze blow across her face was feeling pretty good. She didn't want the honeymoon to end, but then again, she was ready to see her family. Reaching around she hugged her new husband tighter as they made their way out of the village toward the cliffs.

The steep cliffs were giving way to the rocky shores. Just beyond was the white sandy beach. Tonya and Pete would be there in time for sunrise. The ride was magnificent as both glanced over the thirty-foot drop as the water from high tide was slowly making its way back to the ocean.

Tanya spoke into Pete's ear, telling him how much she loved him. Pete turned his head and said he loved her too. As they made their way around the final bend to the beach, Tanya's eyes got wide as she noticed the car coming in their direction. Pete tensed as he saw it too. The car was swerving and headed straight for them. Pete looked left, then to his right over the cliff. There was no way he would be able to pass the car and make it to the brush on the right side of the road. His only chance was to the right and over the cliff. "Hold on tight" Pete yelled to Tanya as he accelerated towards the cliff. The car missed their rear tire by inches as they made their way over the cliff.

Now airborne and twenty feet above the ocean, Pete releases the handles of the scooter and lets it drop to the ocean. He again tells Tanya to hold on tight and try to let her feet hit the water first.

The drop to the ocean seemed to last forever. Pete hit the water first, Tanya came in shortly after. Pete held Tanya's arm and put an arm around her waist as they descended to the bottom. He looked up, tightened his grip on Tanya and pushed hard toward the surface. Breaking the surface, Pete looked to Tanya; she was shaken but didn't seem to be injured. Pete looked toward the shore knowing that the high tide was making way for low tide and they would soon be swept out to sea. So he did what he was taught during his Coast Guard training and swam parallel to the shore.

On the shore a rescue team was quickly formed. The few islanders were in the water moments after Pete and Tanya hit the water. Rickety old fishing boats headed for the ocean, changed their course to make it to the newlyweds. The couple was now weary and treading water. Tanya who swallowed a lot of water was now showing signs of exhaustion. Pete continued to talk to Tanya, telling her to keep fighting, don't quit. He told her he was proud of her. They were staying afloat on pure adrenaline.

A raft pulled close to the couple and tossed a life preserver. Pete reached out for it and quickly secured Tanya. He yelled for the people to get Tanya in the boat and come back for him. He told Tanya that he'll be fine and she needed to let go of him and go to the raft. What she did next surprised him.

She yelled "NO, I am not leaving you, not now not ever. Either we get on that raft together or we keep floating in this water. I am not letting you go!"

He saw the tears in her eyes. She was determined to stay with him. She was clutching his shirt in her fist. He kissed her and said; "I won't leave you, let's make it to the raft" He put on a brave face and gave her a confident smile.

In reality, he wasn't confident he could make it to the raft. He doubted that he could hold on much longer. He had swallowed a lot of water and his chest was heavy. He broke his ankle on impact when they hit the water and his wrist was swollen the size of a grapefruit. He knew he was running out of gas and soon would pass out.

He loved Tanya so much at this moment. He was proud of her. He knew she was now safe, but it would take all he had to make it to the tiny raft. There was no way the tiny Islanders could pull his mass on the raft when he got there, but no way would he tell his wife. He was happy that Tanya would be safe once on the raft. She would live, he was doubtful if he would make it.

Tanya still had his shirt, tugging him along. The skinny islanders were surprisingly strong and seemed to to pull him and Tanya's weight on the preserver with no problem.

He felt his eyes closing and he was about to give up and let go.

He felt a tug on his shirt and hair being pulled from his chest. Tanya was yelling "don't you give up on me, I need you, please baby, don't you give up!"

"I won't, I will not give up, and we're going to make it" Pete said as they reached the tiny raft.

The islanders told Tanya that she had to let go, but she refused. She was trying with all her heart to pull Pete into the boat. The bigger islander finally pulled her hands away and told her to let them handle it. She fell to the bottom of the tiny raft crying.

Pete went under water again. The smaller islander was now in the water somehow keeping him afloat. Pete looked at the smaller guy. The smaller guy smiled at him and said hold on mon, I got you.

Pete asked, "how are you holding me up?'

The little man said with pride "I am the smallest, but strongest man in the village. I am the best swimmer too. You are lucky I happened to be along. Lay your head back and I will pull you to the jet ski coming. Relax mon, I got ya. Your woman is safe in the boat, I promised her I would keep you safe and I never break a promise"

With that Pete laid his head back and fell into a deep sleep.

CHAPTER 31

SPRAIN

The call from Jamaica came in a little before ten in the morning. It was the operator and she wanted to patch a call through. Uncle Len told them to patch the call through and he would pay any charges if needed.

Uncle Len got a serious look on his face and said to no one in particular. "Shouldn't they be in the air by now? Their flight was at nine"

Everyone was sitting in the kitchen. The plan was Grammy and Len would pick up mama and Mr. Pete from the airport when they arrived at seven tonight.

Grammy had sobered up and was drinking coffee at the table. Michael was eating an apple fritter and reading the paper. Me, Rodney, Regina and Ty were playing a serious game of Tunk. We looked over at Uncle Len who was holding the phone to his ear and not saying anything, just nodding. He rubbed his huge mitt of a hand down his face; it looked like he was crying. He said into the phone "Yes Constable I see, thank you for the call.

He pulled up a chair and set it next to Grammy. He sat down and held her hand and put his arm around her shoulder.

Len always took his time when he had something serious to say. So we waited.

He slowly said "mama, kids, I have some bad news to tell you. Tanya and Peterson were in an accident. Seems the scooter they were riding was accidentally ran off the road. Tanya and Peterson went into the ocean. They were swept up by the current and pushed out to the open waters of the ocean. The waters were rough and the current was strong. Peterson being in the Coast Guard and a great swimmer somehow kept himself and your mother afloat. The people on the cliff and the rescuers in the water said that each time they would get close to them, the strong tide would carry them farther and farther out to sea. The Jamaicans had rescue boats and onlookers on the cliffs spotting in case Tanya and Peterson either came ashore or how far they washed out to sea. After a half hour they were spotted in the ocean, the rescuers went to them fighting the rough sea and hauled them into the raft and later on a jet ski. Peterson had tied their belts together, so that they would not float apart. The men who rescued them said that your mama was in Peterson's arms the whole time. He said that they each had one arm wrapped around the others waist and they were holding hands with their finger entwined. The rescuers said the way that they were holding each other that it looked like they were dancing. They were both taken to the hospital and the doctors immediately went to work on them. Doctors said that right now things are looking dim. He said it was up to them to fight, they swallowed a lot of water. The doctors are optimistic and couldn't make any promises. The best we can do is pray for now.

Uncle Len held Grammy tight and quietly broke down. I wasn't sure what it all meant until Rodney said softly "Kim, your mother and Pete are fighting for their lives. Next thing I knew we were all at the table crying and comforting each other. Grammy looked at Ty who was just staring at nothing.

Grammy shook Ty and asked "Baby, are you alright." she thought maybe Ty was in shock.

"Grammy, they were found in each other's arm, that is so beautiful. Mr. Pete always made mama so happy. I am happy that she found a special person who loved her. He said that he would always be there for her and he was there. He kept his word, he didn't lie to her. Grammy, they are going to be just fine, I know that they will" With that said, Grammy took Ty in her arms and Ty gave us all a smile that said everything would be just fine.

I looked at my family and then at Rodney. I couldn't cry, I didn't want to cry. I was devastated at the thought that my mama could somehow not come back to us. Poor Rodney, I held on to him tight. I rocked him in my arms. We all were right there at the table, in each other's arms. That was how we stayed for hours. No one moved, no one said a word. Finally, Grammy put her hands out and we prayed.

I couldn't just sit at the table. I needed to get up for a moment.

I excused myself and made my way to the bathroom.

I splashed water on my face and looked in the mirror. I remembered mama saying how much she loved Mr. Pete and how happy he made her. I could still see the smile on her face each time she said his name. The way they looked at each other, you would think that they were about to melt into each other arms and become one. It used to scare me that she loved him so much and fell for him so hard. Then I realized that he fell for her just as hard and loved her just as much. I smiled at myself in the mirror. I was proud of myself for bringing them together.

The way Mr. Pete would look at her, touch her and kissed her, gave me hope that mama was once again alive inside and able to be happy. I remembered their vows of neither letting the other go, ever. The vow of loving each other in this life, into the next and throughout eternity is a beautiful thing. They were madly in love with each other and it was beautiful.

I found myself smiling at the image of mama and Mr. Pete in the ocean, tied to each other by their belts, hand in hand. I guess love really does conquer all.

I walked back towards the kitchen and paused in the living room. I watched my family for a moment. I knew my mama was watching and would expect us to be strong, not just for her, but as a family.

I slowly made my way to mama's room and knelt at the foot of her bed. I prayed to the heavens and God almighty like I never prayed before. I prayed until I couldn't think of anything else to pray about. Please Lord, I have never asked for anything, only to give thanks, but please return my mama to us and I will …. I will …. I will love her and appreciate her with all my heart.

I crawled up on the bed and pulled back the covers and lay in the spot mama would always lie. I pulled the covers over my head and curled into a ball. I hugged her pillow tight. For the first time in my life I was scared, really scared. Fear struck me and I was frozen. At that moment I wanted my mama more than ever. I needed my mama and I was afraid to move without her. I was suddenly exhausted. I pushed the covers down to my waist and took a long look around the room. I wasn't sure what I was looking for, so I sat and tried to sort it out. I felt the urge to close my eyes, but knew that if I did the tears would start and never stop. So, I stared at the family pictures on her dresser drawer. I thought about the last fight me and mama had. The things I said and didn't mean. How I had been so damn pig headed, selfish and unreasonable. I was such a brat. I deserved the slap mama gave me. I touched my face, expecting to feel the burn.

I could now feel mama's hand on me. Instead of the pain of a harsh slap, mama's hand was softly playing with my hair, delicately cupping my cheeks and she kissed me lightly on the forehead. She was nose to nose with me, looking in my eyes, calling me her little ball of fire and we both were laughing. Mama was telling me all was forgiven and that we were cool.

I inhaled deeply and could smell mama's scent on her pillow. I held the pillow tighter and felt myself drifting off to sleep. I let go and didn't fight the oncoming sleep. Praying that when I woke, this would have been a bad dream and mama and Mr. Pete would walk through the door.

Peterson Mitchell woke up, not knowing where he was or how he got there. He ached from head to toe. Just off to the left of his bed were hanging IV packets. To the right of him were machines whirling, beeping and buzzing. His head was pounding and his throat was dry. He tried calling out, but all he felt was a terrible sore throat. He lifted his right hand to rub his head and there was a soft cast on his wrist. His left leg was in a cast and elevated a foot or so off the bed in a sling. With all of this going on, he was happy that he was still alive.

If he was here, where was His wife Tanya. He looked around the room. The only other bed in the room was empty. He was so sure that when he put Tanya in the raft that she was alive and would survive. If anything happened to her, he would never forgive himself.

A tear rolled down his face and fell softly on the pillow.

He tried again to yell, but nothing came out. He looked around the room looking for something to make noise with. There was nothing, he felt all alone. He looked around the room and there it was above his head, just to his right, the call button. He pushed it and held down for what seemed like minutes. Finally, a portly woman came through the door carrying a bowl of crushed ice and a glass of juice.

"Well hello there Mr. Peterson Mitchell, I'm Patricia. Welcome to the land of the living. Please don't try to talk yet, not until you had some ice and something to drink. You swallowed quite a few liters of salt water and you were extremely dehydrated. Here ya go mon, try dis. She felt his head and fed him a few chips of ice. Her heavy island accent was soothing.

Man did that ice feel good going down Pete thought. Then she put a straw to his mouth and he drank down the fluid. It was thick and soothing like a milk shake, but not as cold. He laid his head back for a moment then sat up on his left arm and tried to speak. Patricia was checking the machines and was beginning to change one of the IV bags.

166

"Excuse me" He said not sure if his voice actually worked this time. It must have because Patricia looked his way. "Excuse me Patricia, where is my wife? Did she, you know make it?"

"Tanya, yes sir mon, she made it. She will be just fine. That one there, she is a fighter and such a beautiful woman"

"Patricia, where is my wife now?" Pete asked

"Sorry mon, where's my manners. Your missus is down the hall in X-ray. Seems she twisted her knee and it needed looking after. She woke about an hour ago, saying she had a twinge of pain shooting up her leg, so I took her to see about it. She will be back real soon"

Patricia reached over and fluffed his pillows and made sure his leg was comfortable. She slowly removed the bandage from his wrist and examined it. She said "This is a nasty sprain, but you will be swinging the tennis racket like Arthur Ashe in no time but the ankle, not so soon. Good thing though, it was a clean break, doctors put it together good as new. Six to eight weeks you'll be dunking the basketball like Doctor J" She gave a hearty laugh.

Pete, feeling a lot better now knowing that Tanya was fine gave a good laugh and told Patricia "The doctor must be really good. If I can play tennis like Arthur Ashe and dunk like Doctor J that would be amazing, seeing how I never swung a racket or dunked a basketball before in my life"

Patricia laughed even louder. Her laugh was infectious and soon Pete was laughing too.

"Mr. Peterson, you are such a funny man. Your wife is funny too. She said to tell you that she needed her leg fixed, so she could kick your ass back to good health. You all are killing me. I'll be back in a moment honey; don't you go anywhere. See I have jokes too. Patricia laughed and left the room.

About ten minutes later Patricia came in pushing Tanya in a wheelchair.

Tanya leapt from the chair and ran to her husband's waiting arms, careful not to hurt his leg.

CHAPTER 32

RODNEY PRICE WAS THE ONE

Today was the day mama and daddy Pete was to return home. It was turning out to be a joyous occasion. It seemed like family and friends were coming out of the wood work. The house was so packed that people overflowed into the back yard. I couldn't tell you how many people showed up, but I do know that all the food we made would probably not last long.

Uncle Len and Grammy called and they were on the way back from the airport with mama and daddy Pete. Uncle Len rented a limo.

Rodney was being the perfect gentleman and a huge help. He was running back and forth to the store for things we needed. He was greeting people at the door. He was also watching over me. I would catch him watching me from across the room and he would give me a little wave. He even brought me a glass of punch and my favorite cookies.

The doorbell rang and since I was the closest to the door, I went to answer it. Rodney appeared and squeezed my hand as I opened the door. My father was on the stoop and he was smiling. I kissed Rodney on the cheek and quietly told him that I needed a moment with my father.

Rodney tapped my shoulder and looked down. I followed his eyes and low and behold, here I had the knife from the cake in my hand. I didn't realize that I had a knife in my hand. I felt Rodney put his hand lightly on my shoulder and say "Kim, give me the knife" He slid his hand down my arm until his hand covered my hand. I smiled at Rodney and reluctantly let the knife go. Rodney took the knife and slowly backed away.

I stepped on the stoop and slowly closed the door behind me. I could have sworn I heard everyone in the house hold their breath. I guess they were waiting for me to go ballistic when they saw daddy on the stoop. Instead I stood on the porch quiet. My father stood on the second step, so I was almost face to face with him. I looked in his eyes and surveyed his haggard face. Life wasn't kind to him. His eyes were like mine and we had a similar nose. Today I was four inches shorter than him and about thirty pounds lighter. Drugs had him wasting away. It's a shame how liquor and fast living can suck the life out of a man. He looked terrible and smelled of cheap cologne and cigarettes. I stood quietly sizing him up. In the back of my mind I was wondering if I lunged for his throat, could I choke the shit out of him before one or all of the party goers stopped me.

Instead of violence, I chilled. I showed a calmness that not only surprised him, but it surprised me as well. I have to say it was a calmness that was a cross between Sidney Portier in the heat of the night telling the white man "they call me Mr. Tibbs!" and Clint Eastwood asking "do you feel lucky, punk? Well, do ya?"

I thought for a moment what I was about to say and chose my words carefully. I finally found the words that needed to be said. I spoke these words in a stern manner. "Daddy, you are no longer welcomed in our house. You will not just show up here whenever you please. You tortured my mother mentally and physically for years. I will not let you rob her of the happiness she deserves. The last year has been a pure joy for my mama. She has learned how to

170

live again, laugh again and trust again. She now loves a man that is good to her in every way. Not only is she there for him, he is there for her.

Daddy, you are a narcissist who will never understand love, commitment and sharing. You were a terrible husband and a rotten father. Mr. Peterson Mitchell took your place and is the only man in my mama's life now. Mama set you free a year ago, now you must go. Daddy, she forgave you, she set you free, time for you to fly away.

Before you turn and walk out of our lives forever, I want you to know a few things. I can never forgive you for how you treated my mama. I can never forgive you for letting my brother and sister down. They wanted you to be their father, but all you were was a failure. I will never forgive you for how you treated me. You hit me, called me nasty names and never had a kind word to say. I always thought I had done something to you to make you hate me. Then I looked in the mirror and saw that I looked just like you. You didn't hate me, you hated you. Because I looked just like you, you could never love me because you hated you.

Mama says I need to forgive you and forget the past, because you are my father.

Really? Forgive you for all the bad shit you did to me over the years, because you are my father?

I don't think so; you've never been a father to me. You are just a man who I will never forgive and I will never ever forget. I will remember you as an example of how to never treat people.

I hate you with my every being. If given the chance, I will kill you in cold blood one day. Today you are spared. But come tomorrow, next week or some day in the future, I will kill you. This is a promise, not a threat.

My mama would not want me to be ugly in front of the people that are here to wish her and her husband well. I am happy for my mama and my new daddy. I want them to be happy. Your being here would not make them happy. Now please leave before they arrive and pray that I never see you again in life. You can leave now"

My father started to speak, but then thought better of it. He turned and took a step. I thought he might turn around, but he walked off our stoop, down the sidewalk and crossed the street. He paused and looked back at me over his right shoulder. I held my thumb and index finger to look like a gun. I raised my arm, took aim and pretended to shoot him. I smiled when I saw the look in his eyes. What a coward.

I felt a familiar arm wrap around my waist from behind. Rodney rested his chin on top of my head. It was so comfortable when he held me like this, I loved this feeling. I somehow knew this was the sensation that mama got from Mr. Pete. Rodney always knew how to make me so happy.

I turned to face Rodney and with the bottom of my fist, I playfully bopped him on the head. In turn, Rodney gave me a playful punch to the kidney, the same way he would do mama.

As we stood embraced on the porch, I realized that since the day Rodney stepped into our lives, he brought nothing but joy to what was an unhappy home. He mellowed me out and helped me to have a happy childhood. He was a good friend to my sister and a confidant to my brother. He helped my mama through a lot of the lowest times of her life. He was the only person that was able to get mama out of a funk with a corny joke. Mama told us that Rodney's mother used to make her laugh by telling the same corny jokes. I believe to this day that Rodney's mother sent him to be with us. She sent her only son to look after her best friend in her time of need. I just wish I could have met his mother, she sounded like she was such a beautiful woman.

Rodney brought out the best in my mama and I will be forever in his debt. Mama went through some low times and Rodney Price was the only person who could truly make my mama laugh.

HE MADE MY MAMA LAUGH

EPILOGUE

Mama and daddy Pete returned home from their honeymoon battered and bruised, but happy to be alive. Daddy Pete came out of the ordeal with a broken ankle and bruised wrist. Mama had a twisted knee and bruised ribs. They had to stay on the island for an additional week for observation. The doctors wanted to make sure they would be alright, seeing how they swallowed up half the ocean.

We decided to go all out for the homecoming party. Since the newlyweds were going to be on the island an extra week, we had an extra week to plan. Michael made a beautiful sign that covered the whole porch. Grammy baked cookies, cakes and pies. The rest of us decorated the house inside and out. Uncle Lem surprised everyone by hiring a limo service and going to pick them up from the airport.

The day they came home friends and family were standing under the big sign on the porch. There were so many people that not only were they milling in our yard, but the neighbors yards as well. When that black stretch limo pulled up to the house and the limo driver let them out of the car, mama and Mr. Pete just stood for a while taking it all in. The crowd yelled welcome home before making their way to the car to greet them. I don't think I ever saw mama cry, but today she was crying like a baby and so was Mr. Pete.

The party finally died down in the early morning hours. The last revelers fixed a to go plate and headed out the door, wishing Mama and Mr. Pete the best. The newlyweds were exhausted. Mr. Pete plopped down in the big recliner and mama came from the kitchen and put a cup of coffee and cookies on the table next to him. She sat on his lap. She reached over picked up a cookie, took a bite and fed him the rest. They looked so comfortable and at peace with each other. It was beautiful.

The family gathered in the living room wanting to know all about their near death adventure. Mama started and Mr. Pete jumped right in, from there on they went back and forth like an old married couple telling us everything from the fall from the cliff, to the rescue and finally the last week on the beautiful island. They had pictures to go along with the stories. They showed pictures of the town, the people and the beautiful sunsets. They even had pictures of Regina's Grandparents and their beautiful home.

That night we were a family again and it felt great. After the conversations subsided, mama and Mr. Pete made their way to their bedroom. The rest of us gathered on the porch. Michael, Ty and I decided to walk everyone home. We made the walk to Grammy's, to see her and Uncle Lem home. Rodney was next and finally Regina. Ty piggy backed on Michael's shoulders the rest of the way home.

I went to my room and changed into my night clothes. I made my way to the kitchen to find Michael and Ty eating cookies at the table. I poured myself a glass of milk and joined them. Michael was telling us that he decided to join the Air Force after graduation. He said he planned on traveling the world and maybe one day becomes a pilot. He promised to always keep in touch and said we were welcomed to visit him where ever he was stationed.

He dunked his cookie until it was soggy and slurped it up and we all laughed.

Ty wanted to let us know that the school councilor told her that if she could keep her grades up throughout high school, she would definitely be able to get an academic scholarship. Ty was beaming and told us that she wanted to go to school in Boston or New York. She wanted to major in finance or international marketing. It sounded so exciting.

They were now looking at me. I looked up from my cookies and milk and innocently asked them "what?"

In unison they asked "what are you going to do with your life?"

Truth was I had never thought about it. My grades were average. I was decent in sports, but I was definitely not a stand out. I liked our little area of town and would never think about leaving, unless of course Rodney left, then where ever he went, I would probably follow. I wasn't sure, I was happy with the way things were. I knew I would have to tell them something, so I sat up straight and said "I want to be a hit woman or a detective like Christy Love. I wouldn't mind killing people for money and living way out in the country"

Instead of laughter and ridicule, they looked at each other shaking and nodding their heads in agreement saying "Hit woman, yeah definitely a hit woman. You would make one bad ass hit woman."

Michael mashed down our afros and rubbed our heads telling us how proud he was to have two cool little sisters. He told us that whatever we did in life he had our backs one hundred percent. Me and Ty stepped over to his chair and gave him a big hug and a kiss. We told him he was the best big brother ever.

....

My father, I let him live for now.

Michael did join the Air force and did become a pilot. Not a fighter pilot, but he pilots the big cargo carrier planes. He now lives in Germany with his beautiful wife, two daughters and a handsome son.

Ty went on to college at Dartmouth; she received a full ride scholarship in academics and basketball. She is an international broker and spends time in between Boston and Paris, France. She is happily married with a precious daughter, a handsome son, two dogs and a cat.

Regina went on to college at Dartmouth. She also received a full ride scholarship in academics and track. Who knew that her feet could move faster than her mouth. She is a writer and foreign correspondent. She also resides in Boston and travels extensively to Paris, London and Germany.

Grammy and my grandfather renewed their wedding vows. Come to find out they were never divorced. The lawyer they hired never filed the paper work. The lawyer told them that they were such a nice couple, he would wait a few days and then file the paperwork, but he lost the paperwork and was too embarrassed to tell them.

Mama and daddy Pete bought a condo on the island where they honeymooned. They spend a few months a year on the island. Mama spends her time on the island searching for interesting art, trinkets and island jewelry. Daddy Pete has taken up painting and photography. They now have shops on three islands and two in Ohio.

Now for Rodney and I. Rodney became an accountant and I joined Army Special Forces. After a few years I grew tired of killing for Uncle Sam and Rodney bored to tears being an accounting clerk. We tried dating, but it just wasn't us. We lived together for a while, but just never got the hang of it. We are better at being friends who take life as it comes. We live a few miles apart in Nashville. He's city, I'm country. We see each other almost every day. After a lot of prodding and pushing, I finally talked Rodney into being a private detective. Me, I do what I do best, I am a hit woman. Rodney is like a superhero, he takes on cases for the good people of the community to make sure justice is served. If he investigates and finds justice isn't served fairly, then he calls on me. Let's just say that he is a vindictive detective and I am his hit woman.

Wow, Rodney and I fighting crime together. I definitely didn't see that coming.

www.ingramcontent.com/pod-product-compliance
Lightning Source LLC
Chambersburg PA
CBHW061137200626
46817CB00016B/1707